Girl in the Mirror

Girl in the Mirror

Jack Lynch

Noriko and Kevin —
I hope you like the stories;
it was fun to write them.
Keep in touch,
Jack

R&Q Press

GIRL IN THE MIRROR
short stories by Jack Lynch

R&Q
Press Inc.

Jack Lynch

Copyright 2010 by Reed and Quill Press

No part of this publication may be
reproduced or transmitted in any fashion
including being stored or moved into
any retrieval system, transmitted by any
means or form including electronic,
photocopying, digital, recording, mechanical,
or any other copying method without
prior written permission of this
book's publisher and copyright owner.

Published by Reed and Quill Press, Inc.
170-13 29th Avenue
Flushing, New York 11358
RnQPress@aol.com

ISBN: 978-0-9825492-9-2
Printed in the United States of America

ALL RIGHTS RESERVED

*For my
lovely Sigrid*

Contents

Introduction
by Dr. Carlos Hiraldo
1

Salud
9

A Birthday
25

The Motel Room
41

Johnny Grows Up
51

The Ferry
59

Carmen
69

The Visit
79

Introduction

by Dr. Carlos Hiraldo

*P*op-cultural representations of New York City almost always miss the mark. They never capture the sweet, grainy pulse of the city — that mixture of wealth and decadence, high-art and low-brow, sleek steel cosmos, trash-hewn ghettos, and leafy small towns that has fascinated and repelled the rest of the country and much of the world since the Dutch ruled its precincts. Following a long period when New York City stood in black-and-white films as a shorthand setting for glamorous sophistication, movies like *Fort Apache in the Bronx* (1981) and *The Warriors* (1979) responded to white flight by falsely portraying the city as a foreign land of imminent danger — a Fallujah of the post-Camelot years undermining the "land of the free" from within. Perhaps in reaction to this unfair image, native son Woody Allen presented an upper-class homogenized New York City in his masterful films of the '70s and '80s. In Allen movies like *Annie Hall* (1977) and *Hannah and Her Sisters* (1986), the still diverse and charged streets of pre-Bloomberg Manhattan spaces like the Upper West Side and Midtown undergo a process of ethnic cleansing. A sea of white, upper-class white at that, is all the viewer sees. Spike Lee in his energetic early period more truthfully captures the ethnic diversity of the City in the 1990s. However, his New Yorkers are not so much human representations as they are political agitprop, less concerned with the details of their everyday lives than with rehearsing their racial grievances and exacerbating inter-ethnic tensions.

Even before 9/11 made it clear to most Americans that New York City was indeed an integral part of the country, television welcomed it back as a safe emblem of cosmopolitan America. In television shows like *Friends* and *Sex and the City*, we get a deracinated New York accessible to Middle America. *Friends* gives us a group of white young adults who manage to live in clean, spacious apartments despite their perennial underemployment. *Sex in the City* meanwhile pretends that an advice columnist in Manhattan can live the life of an heiress without devastating consequences to her credit score and her self-esteem. These shows are more positive representations than the ones Hollywood concocted back when the rest of the country was telling New York City to drop dead, but they are clear examples that the mass media just doesn't get it.

It takes more thoughtful and subtle artistic forms to accurately capture the voracious, loud, contradictory city at the mouth of the Hudson River. Books have traditionally done a better job than any other format. From F. Scott Fitzgerald's *The Great Gatsby* (1925), an ode to the masters of Jazz era New York, to works like Abraham Cahan's *Yekl* (1896) and Jack Agüero's *Dominoes and Other Stories of the Puerto Rican* (1993), collections that show us the struggles of newcomers, narrative fiction has captured the complexities of the great metropolis by focusing on the specific segments that make up the whole.

Following this tradition, Jack Lynch's *Girl in the Mirror* captures an oft-forgotten segment of New York City. The stories in this collection are set in the hardscrabble milieus of bars, old tenements, and cracked sidewalks of Queens and Brooklyn where working-class

Introduction

whites and ethnic minorities comingle. His characters are hustlers because whether through legitimate or illegitimate undertakings if one is not rich, one must hustle to stay afloat in the City. They are white old timers, their impressionable and their disillusioned offspring, young Latinos, and recent immigrants all seeking a better life, one that will not leave them empty amidst so much promise and despair. Instead of struggling for this better world in the midst of their dilapidated neighborhoods, they find the quick fix that usually leads to greater trouble: the ecstasy of alcohol washed away, leaving behind lonely boozers who only feel at home in dark neighborhood bars, and the delirium of lust that confuses itself with love and ends in desperate compromises.

The characters in *Girl in the Mirror* can't be called losers because they haven't given up yet. They hang on, looking for the promise of sobriety and forsaking it for companionship as Inga does in "Salud," or looking for solace in an image of real love and finding greater forms of betrayal as Carmen does at the hands of Johnny and Stan. Disillusionment, as faced by Carmen and the Johnnies of "A Birthday" and "Johnny Grows Up," turns to speed bumps in lives that could be bleak if it wasn't for the eternal light of hope. In their quest for that moment, person and/or place that will turn their lives around for the better, Jack Lynch's characters are quintessentially American types. They search for the all-American promise of starting over as their opportunities continue to dwindle. We see this in Tessie's attempt to commit to Dino in "The Motel" and her decision that a flight to Vegas to work in the casinos, an escape that heralds as much danger as promise, is the only way to deal with his rejection. We also find this continued faith in whatever comes next despite the reality of diminishing returns in Red Kelly's insistence in "The Visit" that someday he will hit the lucky horse.

Only in the main character of "The Ferry," old man Eddie, do we find someone who admits he is at the end of his rope. He is a hard-drinking loner, a man who has aged before his time. He is not counting on the big payoff or the saving romantic relationship to arrive.

However, the plot of the story itself dealing with Eddie's chance encounter with Homer and an invitation to dinner in Staten Island embodies hope. As a reader, one has reason to hope that Eddie's dinner with Homer's family and particularly his subtle connection with Athena, Homer's mother, will revitalize Eddie's spirit and lead him to the realization that human life is about more than mere existence, it is about real connections with other human beings.

Human connection is what we all want and what the characters in Lynch's *Girl in the Mirror* seek mostly in vain. Alcohol, that social lubricant that since ancient times has promised us joy and Dionysian companionship, becomes a crucial character in these stories. It is the central theme of "Salud," the introductory story of the collection. Inga and Bob are two alcoholics wrestling with the realization that drinking will destroy their lives but fearing sobriety as a dry unimaginative space. They meet in a bar when Inga gets locked out of the halfway house in which she stays to dry out. Their connection throughout the night, emotional rather than physical, depends more on what they lack than on what they can offer each other. Though Inga is at the edge of regressing into alcoholism and Bob appears to be in denial about his own problems with liquor, the tone of the story is surprisingly hopeful. The ending leaves open the real possibility that Inga can walk away from alcohol and from Bob's self-delusion as she declines his invitation to continue drinking. However, the "I'll call you" from Bob that marks the end of the story, normally a Romantic denouement, also hints at the possibility that Inga's desire to connect with Bob will be her undoing.

Similarly, in "A Birthday," alcohol promises to connect the twelve-year-old narrator to the adult world of his father and his father's friends when he is invited to join them in drinks. Instead of finding camaraderie, however, Johnny discovers the treachery and betrayal underlying adult lives as he stumbles into dark secrets kept by his father and his associates. Jim, the reticent young adult of "The Visit," comes across as a wizened, often disillusioned version of the twelve-year-old Johnny. He attends school, dates an Afro-

Introduction

Brazilian girl despite his staunchly proud Irish-American's father disapproval, and only humors his dad enough to stay in contact with him. The scene at the bar, where Red Kelly keeps drinking at his son's expense despite Jim's obvious discomfort with the atmosphere, exposes the exhausted residue of the joy and conviviality that little Johnny expected to find when he went drinking with his father in "The Birthday."

If alcohol is not a central feature of other stories in Lynch's *Girl in the Mirror* it is in the background of tales like "The Motel," "The Ferry," and "Carmen." The reader gets the sense that whatever issues and troubles these characters once had have been exacerbated by a reliance on alcohol to dull pain, to create excitement, and to make fleeting encounters seem more significant. Certainly one comes from "The Ferry" with the clear understanding that alcohol lies as a central cause of Eddie's hollow existence. Moreover, in Tessie and Carmen we get two working-class New York women who depend on alcohol and men for their fulfillment. The former, of course, serves as the conduit for mistakes with the latter. Both Tessie and Carmen rely on older men for financial and emotional support. They are dismissive of these more mature lovers while they seek true affection in young men who are not ready for commitment. Tessie's Dino is an old-fashioned "mook." He expects nothing but a life of manual labor, nights of hanging out with friends, and casual encounters with women. When he discovers Frank, the other man in Tessie's life, his masculine ego is enraged but not enough to fight for her love. As mentioned above, Tessie's claim at the end of "The Motel" that she will go to Las Vegas with her friends can be read either as a harbinger of renewal in the West, as a foreshadowing of pending disaster in the more permissive city where alcohol and casual encounters are more readily available, or simply as an empty threat from a character who has never spent much time outside New York City. Though Carmen has more pep and vigor than Tessie, one gets the feeling her possibilities are even more limited. While dismissing the affections of the older Angelo, she continues to think of the newly married Stan as "the love of her life." In a futile attempt to seek revenge on the man who has rejected her, Carmen seduces Johnny, Stan's best friend. The unexpected twist at the end of "Carmen" is both funny and heartbreaking, a complex conclusion that attests to Lynch's considerable narrative skills.

Jack Lynch is a native New Yorker and a lifelong resident. The author of *Manhattan Man and Other Poems*, his 2008 collection of original poems, Lynch has the City in his bones. He knows New York City in a way that transplants with artistic dreams wish they did. Its structure is the structure of Lynch's mind. Much like the city streets, Lynch's stories build with suspense, promise, and menace in every opening. The tone, the scenes, and what's left unstated by the characters whets the reader's appetite for more. Every line, like every corner of the great metropolis, becomes pregnant with the possibility of success or disaster for the main characters of these stories. Lynch creates spare, hard worlds that in the hands of a lesser writer would only serve to provide social messages or create losers for us to gawk at. In Lynch's hands, we get the story of complex working-class New Yorkers whose dreams and schemes for a better life we can all empathize with. His endings are never fully happy or completely tragic. They leave us suspecting that these characters will continue to have ups and downs as they continue to seek meaning in their lives.

The classic Frank Sinatra song tells us about New York that "if I can make it there, I can make it anywhere." But what happens to those who don't "make it"? What happens to those who do not become the millionaires, the celebrities, and supermodels the media assumes all honest New Yorkers to be? What about the ordinary New Yorkers, who own small shops, drive buses and trains, attend school, and drink their blues away at the neighborhood bars? Hollywood would have us believe that if you live in this city of millions and you are not a trust fund intellectual, a Wall Street tycoon, a celebrity, or a hardened criminal, you don't exist. Jack Lynch's *Girl in the Mirror* brings to life the anonymous engine of New York City, the folks that

Introduction

make it march and go and give it its true color in good and bad times. I invite you now to read these stories. You will discover New Yorkers who are as real and as American as you.

Salud

She was in Macy's that evening when the snow began to fall. She could see the snow coming down by the entrance of the department store. There were hundreds of little snowflakes swirling around and they reminded her of little white feathers. She remembered herself as a very young child sleigh-riding down a long winding hill with her father. The snow that late afternoon was coming down heavy as they made their way down the hill. Her father always had plenty of hard candies to give her when they got to the bottom. She remembered the excitement and fear as her father steered the sled down Dead Man's Hill. They laughed and laughed until they fell off the sled into the snow. She loved everything about winter, even the very cold days. Inga checked her watch. She had been walking around Macy's for quite a long time. She was right on schedule. She still had plenty of time before getting back to the shelter.

Of all the department stores in Manhattan Inga liked Macy's the best because when she was married to Roger, she worked there as a salesgirl. Inga remembered walking into the store early in the morning, clocking in and talking to the other girls. At that time she was impressed by her manager, Mrs. Spatafora, who was in charge of the fourth floor. Inga thought she was the most perfectly dressed woman she had ever seen. Everything was in place including her shiny black hair.

Inga loved spending time in the make-up department trying on all the different cosmetics and sometimes they would give her a free make-up consultation. Macy's gave her a wonderful and positive feeling, although she did have some fears. One of them was that she would run into someone she knew, someone she had worked with or a manager she had worked for. How would she explain her present circumstances? Would they be able to tell that something was wrong with her? Maybe they wouldn't respect her and say something awful to her. After strolling around the first floor and seeing all the new cosmetics, she checked her watch again and realized that it was getting late. She had to hurry. The nuns at the shelter were great and very supportive to her. They encouraged her to explore the Big Apple. Even though she had been brought up in New York City there was still so much to see. She explained to the nuns that when you are born here you take everything for granted. For example, she had never been to the Statue of Liberty or even to the top of the Empire State Building. Now she had to get to the subway because the one thing they strictly enforced was being back on time. If she was not there by 10 P.M. she would be locked out. They had locked out Kathy last week. There were no exceptions. She realized that they had to be like that because if someone came back drunk or stoned they would disturb and upset the others. She was grateful for that.

On the subway Inga sat facing a large woman with a big tattoo of a broken heart on her neck. Becoming so engrossed with the large woman and the crying child sitting next to her she missed her stop. She had to get off at the next stop, cross over the platform, wait for the subway going back to her station and then hurry to the shelter which was all the way on Tenth Avenue. The snowflakes were whirling wildly in the wind and a little slush was forming making it slippery in spots. She had to make sure she didn't slip and fall down.

By the time she arrived at the shelter, the doors were locked. It was after 10 P.M. She knocked hard but no one came to the door. No room at the inn, she thought. Everybody is nice and cozy inside and I'm on the street again. Inga Marie Anderson with nowhere to go.

Salud

She sat down on the steps, which were protected from the snow by a green canopy. She wanted to crawl into a cot and fall asleep. She wanted to wake up in the morning to have breakfast with the nuns and her friends.

She was beside herself. How had she let this happen? Inga looked around her and then slowly got up and headed toward a flash of light that came from a diner. She entered the diner and went to one of the stools and ordered a coffee. Next to her was a girl with a long ratty fur coat and work boots. She was talking to a young guy with dirty black hair and a worn frayed flannel shirt. When the girl stopped talking and took a sip of her tea, she turned to Inga and asked her what she was doing out on a night like this.

"I'm staying at a place down the street and I got locked out." The girl gave her a sad smile giving Inga the feeling that this girl had been through something similar in her life. Then the girl surprised her by giving her ten dollars, "Get yourself a burger to go with the coffee honey. It's on me." Then she turned to the guy and started talking excitedly about a play that she was going to audition for.

"Thank you," Inga said to the girl's back.

Now she had to figure out what to do next. She hovered over her coffee for at least ten minutes wondering if she should order the burger or not. Maybe if she didn't order the burger, the girl would take her money back. Surprisingly, the couple suddenly left without even saying goodbye. Inga spent another ten minutes thinking about what to do and sipping her coffee. She pictured her and her ex-husband, Roger, how they loved diners. They would eat at a different diner whenever they went out, followed by a nightcap at their favorite bar. They once had a beautiful apartment in Queens and then he had to relocate. Inga had loved him so much. While she waited in New York for him to get settled, he met another woman and soon thereafter he told Inga that he wanted a divorce. He broke her heart. Maybe it was the drink that did it. Never blaming him, always excusing him. She finished her coffee and went outside.

She started walking toward the East Side. She knew where she needed to go. She wanted a drink. Thinking about Roger was not a good idea. Maybe after a drink she could sort things out. When she got to Madison Avenue, she saw a bus heading uptown, and she pictured Nat's Place. It was never ever crowded in there and she knew the bartender Harry would leave her alone. She got on the bus and sat by the window on the left side. The thought entered her mind that she couldn't remain at the shelter forever.

She closed her eyes to escape everybody, but her mind dialed up the picture of Roger once again. There he was dancing with her at that beautiful nightclub in Barbados. They had chosen a wonderful resort for their honeymoon and the nightclub was right across the street. He was telling her how he loved her and how happy he was that she was in his life. Inga let out a big sigh and opened her eyes. She couldn't take any more of that. As she looked out the window she saw the blank faces of the mannequins in expensive dresses and suits in the stores of Madison Avenue. She felt empty and listless like those mannequins. After she got off the bus on 55th Street she walked down to Third Avenue. There it was beckoning to her, Nat's Place.

When Harry placed a glass of red wine before her she felt better. She did not want to drink it but somehow she knew she would. She pretended that she was interested in looking at the bottles behind the bar. Inga began to look for Laird's Apple Jack, a whiskey made from apples that Roger loved. She started fidgeting with some papers in her pocketbook — the only thing of importance to her right now and started reading an old letter from her sister. Almost involuntarily, her hand picked up the glass. Carefully, she returned it to the counter. Then she began looking at herself in the mirror of the bar, as if the person in the mirror were someone else. She touched her glass tenderly, and then turned it around. She went back to reading her sister's letter. She returned to the glass, sliding it slowly back and forth. When she finally raised her glass, she could no longer fool herself; her hand was shaking when she placed her lips on the tip of the glass. Why was she doing this now?

Her drink was almost finished so she picked up the *News* that

Salud

was lying on the stool next to her. The wind brought a cold draft into the bar and before she knew it a handsome man in his fifties with kind blue eyes, a wrinkled forehead, and a sweet smile was standing at her side, "Hey, where's your boots, sweetheart?"

"I left them in Michigan where they have real snow storms. Where's your shovel?" she laughed.

"Hey, you're quick with the words. I got to watch you."

She thought he may have had a few drinks before he came in. He was wearing an expensive top coat and when he took it off she was surprised to see a suit and a tie on the man. He continued talking, "You know, the more I look at you, the more I think I recognize you."

"Oh, my goodness, that's some line you have."

"No, I'm serious."

"I think you had a few drinks too many."

"Well, yes I did. I just went off the wagon."

"Me too! Just now."

"Oh, that's where we met!"

"Where?"

"At an A.A. meeting. We didn't actually meet but I recognize you. You had a little red hat on like you're wearing now."

"Wow, you got a good memory." Inga looked at her glass of wine.

"Don't worry," he winked, "I won't tell anyone." He called to the bartender, "Hey, Harry, give me the regular, will you?" He turned to her and said, "We're in the same boat. I'm getting a scotch, a double Dewar's."

They looked at each other. Both in A.A. and both drinking, immediately connected, like two lost souls, she thought.

She finished her wine. "How about a drink for me?"

"Hell no, how long you been in A.A.?"

"About three months, off and on."

"I stayed sober for a year going to many meetings. I can't buy you a drink, honey, but I could always offer you a little pot."

She noticed that he had been staring at her blue eyes and her shoulder-length blond hair.

"Are you Swedish, by any chance?" he asked with a smile.

"No, I have a Norwegian background," she answered simply. "My name is Inga."

"Now, let's see if I remember that saying, 'A hundred Swedes crept through the weeds, chased by one Norwegian.'"

She laughed putting her hand to her lips, "My mother would give you a kiss for that, except it should be twenty Swedes."

"Hey, why don't you give me a kiss instead?"

"You're pretty fresh, aren't you?"

"Well, I've met you twice now — that's like our second date. Besides, if you share some pot with me, we'll be kissing in no time. You know, I really like pot. I used to go up to the attic and do my thing there while my wife was doing the dishes. Maybe my friends in A.A. were right. The pot increased my desire for a drink and I had one yesterday."

She watched him toss the scotch down and then knock on the bar for another. Meanwhile, she nodded to Harry for a refill. The handsome guy continued with his non-stop talk while pulling up a stool next to her, "The problem is that life without a drink is awful. Don't you think so?"

"But you were dry for a whole year."

"A slip can happen at any time honey. Look, aren't you drinking? A relapse is always around the corner, so let's make a toast that tomorrow we will stop. SALUD, which is Spanish for TO YOUR HEALTH."

He clinked his glass with hers and they drank a toast. She brushed her blond hair back with her fingers.

"I'm afraid I'm a true alcoholic. I go from one extreme to another. Sometimes I'm dancing like Zorba the Greek and other times I'm crying in my beer. In the meantime, I feel I know all about you."

His face was filled with sincerity yet he sounded like some kind of salesman or maybe he was just a character. She could size up people right away and he seemed harmless.

Salud

"And I feel I know all about you," she said. "You're a Damon Runyon type of guy."

"Hey, that's pretty good."

"And what am I gonna call you?"

"Call me Blackout Bob. I'm from upstate New York — a little town called Eden, right outside of Buffalo and I fell in love with Holden Caulfield, you know, Salinger's character."

"Yeah, I think I heard about him."

"Well, Salinger just died in January. He lived to the ripe old age of 91. At one time he was considered the most important American writer since World War II. His most important book was called, *The Catcher in the Rye* which shocked and inspired everyone. Holden Caulfield, his most famous character, was a teenager expelled from school who hated phonies and he became more popular than Huckleberry Finn. Holden was a kid who passed himself off as an adult so he could drink. Hey, when I was 15, I disguised myself like he did. I flashed a roll of bills, a ten dollar bill on top, the rest singles and kept my head down at the bar. One morning I woke up and didn't know where my wallet was or how I got home. Good thing an older friend of mine came by to return the wallet and give me a story that I could tell my parents or else I would have been in a kettle of fish. Hey, are you listening to me? Don't fall asleep on me. I got lots more to tell you."

"I'm listening."

"After high school, I found the Marines and thank heaven I met some buddies, drinking buddies. We were stationed in the South and Lamar introduced me to white lightning in a mason jar and my hours of liberty were consumed with country music and drink. Smitty got me to read Hemingway when I was sober; he introduced me to my first wife."

"How many did you have?"

"I had four wives." She signaled Harry to bring her another drink.

"You had four wives? That's enough for any man."

"Listen, I just remembered I have to walk my dog Spotty. You wanna help me? Hey, wait a minute, I'll be right back. You stay here...don't move. I'm going to see a man about a horse." With a wink he headed toward the bathroom.

After Bob left, Harry, the bartender, came over to Inga to tell her that the man at the end of the bar had bought her a drink. She turned around to see who it was. She was disappointed to find out that it was an old drunken coot with a white beard and a ponytail. Trouble, she thought, but it would be a shame to waste a drink. She made a compromise. She'd have his drink, take the remainder of her money on the bar and leave with Bob, but give the old coot a thank you before going out the door.

When Bob returned he greeted her with, "Now where was I, wife number one or wife number two?"

"Tell me about the second one," she sighed.

"But I haven't even told you about number one, but she only lasted four years, dropping me for a chubby bank vice president with money. Can you imagine that? My second wife, which is the one you wanted to know about, was married to another marine buddy named Paul who died suddenly in a car accident. After drinking three days in his honor, his widow Carol and I decided to marry. We lived in a trailer next to a carnival. She used to do the books for the circus people — some of them came from Bulgaria. We lasted a year then she ran off with the strong man when I was drunk. The next morning I had a black out and didn't remember what happened. The clowns had to tell me I was a bachelor again."

Inga managed to finish half of her wine while he was telling that story. Then she spotted the ponytail man heading her way. Time to bail out, she thought. "Hey, let's go and let your dog take a pee, Bob. Maybe we should get going."

He began to put his coat back on while she gulped her wine and took her money.

"I'll leave the tip," he said.

She almost knocked Mr. Ponytail over when she backed off her stool.

"Oh, are you going already?" he asked her drunkenly.

"Yeah, we have to take care of a dog in trouble."

As they walked to the door Bob asked, "Who was he?"

"Some guy at the end of the bar."

"So long, Harry," Bob said as they left Nat's Place. Bob hailed a taxi and soon they were in Greenwich Village. Bob lived in a fifth-floor walk up but fortunately he lived on the second floor. They could hear Spotty crying at the door. Bob quickly opened the door and put the leash on his dog. He introduced Inga to his bulldog, "Spotty, this is Inga our new friend. Be nice to her and please notice she is not a fire hydrant."

Spotty rolled over to show her one of his many tricks. Inga was charmed. After a walk around the block, they returned to the apartment and Spotty headed for his basket by the bookcase. He looked relieved.

They sat on the couch and Bob handed her a printed page — a review of one of his books. She read it out loud and when she finished Bob looked at Spotty who was watching him, "Yes Spotty," he said, "you heard what she's reading. It's about me!" They laughed at the sleepy-looking bulldog.

"This is a terrific review, Bob. You should be very proud of yourself."

"Even my brother Peter liked it. We talk on the phone once a week. He lives in Brooklyn. He wanted me to go to a concert with him this evening but I begged off. Say, have you had anything to eat? Wanna go for a bite?"

"Yes, I'm hungry," she admitted.

They took a cab. It was snowing again. It was slushy and the snow was sticking in some spots and, of course, he started talking to the cab driver about football and the Giants in particular. She leaned for a moment on his arm when getting out of the taxi. She felt tired. It was past her normal hour for sleep. She watched the snowflakes against the neon light of the restaurant on Jane Street in the Village. Marty's Bistro, as she found out had an upstairs restaurant and a downstairs bar. He took her upstairs. There wasn't much of a crowd so they found a table easily. The waiter came and he ordered a gin and tonic for them both. She felt as if she were watching a movie that she had seen before. She knew how it would end.

∽ ∾

She woke up on Bob's pull out couch in the living room. Her head was throbbing and her stomach didn't feel well. The room was dark, but the door was open a fraction to another room where some light filtered out. All she could hear was a ticking clock. Her pillow was soft not like the pillow in the shelter. She ran her fingers through her hair and sat up. She was lying under a white comforter.

Bob must have been in the kitchen. He came over to her. "You're up a little early, honey. How goes it?"

"Not so good."

"I'm not surprised. We drank a lot last night."

He brought her some water and an Alka Seltzer, "Do you want anything else?"

Before she could answer Spotty jumped on the bed and put his paw on her shoulder. She started to laugh, "I'll be all right. Thanks."

Spotty watched her drink the Alka Seltzer.

"I'll be in the next room if you need anything. Maybe you'll be able to get some sleep now."

"Thanks Bob."

When she woke again, sunshine was coming through the window. She sat up and looked around her. There was a beautiful blue rug on the floor and the walls were peach-colored. There was an old fashioned bookcase against the wall opposite her. She went to the bathroom. She took a quick shower, brushed her teeth, and discovered a brown bathrobe on the hook of the door, probably his. She put it on and went back to the living room. Spotty came over to her. She bent down to stoke his head and then Bob came out from the kitchen.

Salud

"I hope you don't mind. I took a shower and put on your bathrobe."

"No, of course not."

"But I don't remember what happened last night after we came back from the restaurant."

"Are you trying to outdo Blackout Bob? Last night you talked about someone following you, someone bothering you."

She remembered sitting on the couch and crying and Bob telling her not to worry so much.

"Last night you talked about your family a lot," he said.

The phone started to ring. The machine picked up and a woman's voice came on, "Hi, this is Nicole and Bob, please leave a message." There was no message.

"Hey, I got a real bad hangover. Maybe I should just leave," Inga said.

"Listen, I have a surefire cure for your hangover. It's a raw egg, tomato juice and a dash of bitters. It will cure the worst hangover and it stops hiccups too. In fact, I think I'll make one for myself."

"I have a better cure. Let's have a drink."

"Okay, not a bad idea. I've got scotch, gin, beer, or wine."

"I don't care. Anyone will do."

Bob left and returned with two glasses of scotch. They drank it quickly.

Inga said, "What if your wife comes back? I think I want to get going now."

"Hey, I'm sorry about that phone business. But you can't leave now. I could let you leave but Spotty would really be upset and anyway we haven't even had breakfast yet. We could go to the diner. You get ready and I'll take Spotty for a walk. I hope you'll be here when I get back."

"Maybe I'll stay for Spotty."

Bob took her to his favorite Greek diner. He stopped to introduce her to George, the owner, and Nicos his son. He also said hello to three people who were sitting at the counter. He put a hand on one shoulder, shook somebody else's hand and touched a woman's cheek. She was hungry watching everyone eat their eggs and pancakes. George led them to a big booth. Kalliope, a heavy woman in her forties with a Greek accent, hurried over to them. "You want coffee, right Bob and your usual, eggs sunnyside and you, what you want?" She looked at Inga suspiciously.

"Kalliope, this is Inga and she'll have the same as me, right, Inga?"

"No, that's too much for me. I'll just have the silver dollar pancakes. My stomach is a little queasy from last night."

Kalliope smiled. "And coffee, right?"

"And coffee, *andoxi.* "

"I like this Inga, Bob. She can speak some Greek, not like you."

Recovering quickly, Bob asked Kalliope, "When are you taking me to Crete so I learn your language?"

"When you marry my daughter Tessie," she laughed and she moved on to the kitchen smiling.

Bob said, "It takes so little time to be kind to people. I love to make people happy. I was raised where people greet each other on the street and talk to strangers, although I haven't been back to my hometown in ages."

He looked sad.

Inga said, "Why don't you go back?"

"I've been here thirteen years and the place has grown on me. It's in my blood. So Inga, how long have you been living at that place?"

"It's my anniversary, three months at the shelter and three months sober until yesterday. The nuns were very good to me and they got me to go to A.A. meetings regularly. They have strict rules, though, and I don't know if they'll let me back."

"Tell them about the snow storm and that you stayed over with a friend. They'll take you back. Don't worry."

Salud

"I'm not so sure."

"Do you have any other place to crash?"

"No."

"Then you could always stay with me."

"What if your wife comes back?"

"She won't. I did this to her too often. She won't be back."

The food arrived and he spent the rest of the time wolfing his meal down while she enjoyed her pancakes. She began to feel much better after eating. When he paid the bill he asked her, "How are your shoes holding up in the snow?"

"They're a little wet but not bad."

"Come on, let's get you some boots!"

They left the diner and headed for a shoe store on Greenwich Avenue. She was in pretty good spirits and when she looked around the store, she saw Bob talking to the salesman. Finally, she spotted a pair of boots she loved. She couldn't believe that he was going to buy her a pair of boots.

Sitting in a chair and having a young man gazing up at you makes you feel like a princess, she thought, that's why shoe stores are a good business. Then she remembered the state of her shoes and socks. She knew that one sock had a hole in it. She delayed taking off her shoes, but the inevitable happened. As soon as Bob saw her sock, he suggested that she buy a new pair. He tried to cover up her embarrassment by saying that he always bought socks when he got shoes. After picking out new socks, she put them on and then put her new boots over them. Inga felt like a new person. She was ready to face the new day.

Bob wanted to go to the movies. He was a movie buff and a local movie house was playing *Gone with the Wind*. Actually, Inga had never seen it and Bob was simply amazed. Even though the movie began at 11:45 in the morning there was a bit of a line waiting to get into the art movie theater near Varick Street. While on the line Inga started to get worried about returning to the shelter. She was also dreading the moment when the theater would grow dark and the film would begin. Maybe Bob would put his arm around her or maybe try to kiss her. Inside, having bought the tickets, he also bought a large tub of popcorn as well so she was a bit relieved. His hands would be occupied with holding the large container. She would just pick at the popcorn. She was also happy that he didn't steer them to the back of the movie house. He asked her where she wanted to sit.

She was surprised there was an intermission. Bob didn't tell her that the movie was almost four hours long. Actually, the first part of the movie moved quickly. Her hangover disappeared and she became completely engrossed with Scarlett. Scarlett was a selfish woman who tackled life with intensity and passion. Even though she was downright mean at times, Inga was still rooting for her to survive.

"Hey, let's go to a place I know for a ginger ale okay? I have a bit of a thirst because of all that popcorn I ate. The place is across the street," he said, stretching his arms.

"Okay," she said.

The bar was bathed in a gentle and soft afternoon light. It was strange being there. Frank Sinatra music was playing in the background and a couple of girls were sitting on stools. They were laughing with the bartender, a skinny kid with an earring and a T-shirt that said, "Drinking is my business." Bob called him and he ambled over. He wasn't in a hurry. "What's up?" he asked. "Give those ladies another round. I'll have a Dewar's on the rocks and Inga will have a ginger ale."

"Hey," Inga said, "we were both going to have ginger ales."

"I'm sorry, I forgot."

"Well then I can change my mind too. I'll have a beer." She could picture Scarlett saying that.

The bartender went to get the girls their drinks.

"I don't know if you should have a beer, Inga."

"And I don't think you should have a Dewar's."

One of the girls with short, curly dark hair raised her glass to

Salud

Bob and yelled, "Gracias. Salud!" The other one, a brunette, just raised her glass in a salute.

"You're welcome. De nada," Bob returned. Then he looked at Inga, "Okay, I'm not going to be a Daddy. You have what you want and I'll have what I want."

The bartender was back. "A beer for the lady and a Dewar's for me," Bob said.

"Right."

The bartender returned with their drinks.

Bob put his arm around her and whispered in her ear, "When are you going back to A.A.?"

With those words she started to cry. She couldn't help it.

"Don't worry, I'll try to help you anyway I can."

"I feel so worthless."

"Hey, I'm here for you. Just get yourself together. I remember reading the poet, T.S. Eliot. Well, he said that people cannot bear very much reality."

After the first round she knew that they were going to miss the rest of the movie.

"Take me back to the shelter," she said.

"Do you want a cup of coffee first?"

"Okay, just coffee. Nothing else."

"What if I have an Irish coffee?"

"It's okay by me. It's your life."

Bob ordered two regular coffees. When the coffees arrived, he said, "Let's have a toast to never drinking again. Salud."

"You're not supposed to say that. One day at a time, remember?"

Bob laughed as he sipped his coffee. After they finished their coffees, he paid the bill. They left the bar and started walking towards the shelter. Not much was said. Inga stopped suddenly, held on to his arm, kissed him on the cheek and whispered, "Thanks for the boots, for everything."

And before changing her mind, she began walking away.

"Hey, Inga, I'll call you."

A Birthday

My father had opened his watch store with his best friend, Stan, on Fifth Avenue twelve years ago, when I was born. Today was a special day because it was my birthday and on this cool September afternoon with clouds moving quickly covering and uncovering a strong four o'clock sun, he was going to tell me a secret. It had to do with the store, Patrick's Place — watches and clocks. When he came up the stairs to fetch me from the apartment, he had fortified himself with a few drinks. My mom reminded him about his promise, something about the birds and bees. My dad replied, "Don't worry, I'll remember."

My mother stood at the door when we left, "Don't forget to come home for your special dinner at seven tonight, Johnny, and bring your father in tow."

My father kissed her with those twinkling eyes of his, "Have I even been late before?"

"Don't give me any of your malarkey, Pat. Just get here on time, and watch out for your son; he's a little too smart for his own good. He's more like twelve going on twenty. And don't forget. Only one drink for your son Patrick."

"Yeah, don't worry."

The store was just two blocks away from our apartment, which was on a side street close to Fifth Avenue. My father warned me that I could never tell anyone about the secret place. To emphasize his words he raised his index finger to his lips. "Mums the word, son." With those words of wisdom, he took his flask of Irish whiskey from his pocket and took a slug. "Don't even tell your best friend, Carmine." Again he raised his finger to his lips. "Not a word, okay?"

"What about Brian and Frank?" I asked.

"No, you can't tell your brothers. This is a secret between you and me. Period."

"What about Kathy and Annette?" I said.

"No, you can't tell your sisters either. They must never know."

"What about Mom then?"

He sighed. "Especially, not your mom. . . this is for men only. Soon you are going to be confirmed. . . that means that you will be a man in the eyes of the church. You must promise me that you will not tell anyone about what you see today."

"Okay, Dad. . . I promise."

We had just approached Murphy's Pub on the corner and my father looked as if he wanted to drop in but I had to give him credit. He passed it right by and he didn't even look in the window. Maybe that was because he had his drink in his pocket. Because I was the only one in the family who cared about his watches, his clocks and his store, my father hoped one day that the store would belong to me. Even though it would be a long time away, it made him happy.

I was raised among watches and clocks. I used to watch my father fix them from the store's window. His work bench was located in the store alongside the front window. At the end of the day at supper he would tell me what time I came by the store to watch him. I would always look over his right shoulder so he wouldn't see me and I wouldn't disturb him. I thought he was a magician of sorts until I found out he had a mirror and he could see who was looking over his shoulder. I caught him once turning around and winking at a lady.

Working by the window was Stan's idea. He was my father's partner, the silent partner, the money man. He really didn't repair the watches and clocks, but he was a natural salesman and could charm

A Birthday

the pants off of anyone. At first, my father didn't want to work by the window but Stan told my father that he would become very famous in the neighborhood. Really, it was just an advertising gimmick to bring in the customers. Stan got the idea from the Greek tavernas that had their kitchens in the front of the store so that upon entering potential customers could get an idea about how the food looked and how it was cooked. The cooks were always cleanly attired because they were on display. Some of the cooks found wives this way.

My father claimed that it was his idea. He got the idea from construction sites. Men always like to watch others work. That's why there are holes bored into the wooden walls of a construction site. Men can look through the holes and comment about how the job is coming along, who is working hard and who is lazy. They even complain to passersby how they could do the job better.

My uncle Harry said it was his idea because people could entertain themselves looking at my father without going into the store to speak to my father or to Stan. If they did they would be bored to death, but if Harry was there they could enter to hear his wonderfully funny jokes. Who knew what the truth was?

At any rate, when my father and I approached the store on this day, actually, my birthday, a small man, Jimmy the Mope, who always reminded me of a troll with his hunchback and his sharp features opened the shutters for us. It was a Sunday and Jimmy was hired to keep an eye on the store because of a recent robbery in the neighborhood. He stared at me and wished me a happy birthday, but I could tell he really didn't care. In silence we followed my father to the back of the shop to the storeroom. It smelled of coffee and was cluttered with clocks, spare parts, and boxes. It was a chaotic place except for one area where a beautiful clock was hung high on a wall. Towards the corner on the right side of the room there was a beat up rug. I had seen it so many times but it was so old and ragged that I never paid it much attention. My father told Jimmy to pull back the rug and there it was — a trap door! Jimmy lifted the trap door by pulling a rusty, round, short handle exposing a flight of old dirty wooden stairs. "Wow! This is exciting," I said. The two men looked at me and laughed at my surprise. Jimmy entered the hole in the floor and walked down some wooden stairs. We followed. My father pushed a hidden button which cast a dull light on a part of the basement which I had never seen. A maze of passageways greeted me and it took me a minute to get used to the dimness of the place pierced by shafts of light that came from the ceiling. We followed one corridor that had steps and platforms. There were libraries of books, storerooms, and clocks all around. My father smiled at me and winked.

"I want you to know that this place was used as a bomb shelter during the fifties when we thought the Russians would attack us. We called it the catacombs, a place of treasures as well as a tomb for the dead bodies of old watches and clocks. There are priceless things down here."

"This place is haunted, too. There are ghosts down here. I won't come down here by myself," Jimmy the Mope stated. My father placed his finger to his lips again motioning to Jimmy that he should not talk.

"Don't listen to Jimmy's superstitions," my father said. I could smell the liquor on his breath. "Listen to me. Each watch and clock down here has a history, a destiny. This is a place of mystery. There are untold treasures here. Each watch and clock is special and today I want you to choose a watch. I want you to adopt it, to clean it, and to never lose it because its destiny will become your destiny. Do you understand? I am going upstairs now. I need to fortify myself. Jimmy will keep an eye on you, but he has made a vow of silence while in this place. He cannot talk to you. Now go find a watch to keep. I'll see you upstairs when you finish your quest."

For over an hour I wandered around the dust-filled cellar. I remembered being in the cellar of a grocery store one time that had one dull light bulb hanging from the ceiling. It was filled with boxes and empty bottles but this was different. That place was filled with

A Birthday

the smell of ripe fruit and vegetables; this place was filled with the smell of wood, oil, old paper, and dust. I coughed for a little while, and then let my hand brush over old, opened desks with cubbyholes filled with watches and parts of watches. There were exposed clocks, too, and exposed cabinets. There were paintings of vampires, werewolves, and strange-looking creatures — half-man and half-animal. There were shelves of large books with pictures of clocks. There were smaller books with dates of companies that produced watches of all kinds. In each part of the place, there were different sounds: chimes from cuckoo clocks, and the sound of the movements of toy animals circling an old grandfather clock. It was eerie and I felt I was walking in a forgotten place, while upstairs in the outside world people were living a normal life counting the ticks of time. I wanted to stay in this place for a long time reading from a book or checking a watch in the cubby hole of a desk. I even enjoyed running my hands over old cabinets and desks, feeling the wood and the carvings of names and places in the nooks of the wood. Suddenly, some loud chimes from an old clock scared the hell out of me. I turned around looking for Jimmy, but he wasn't visible. Was he still around?

I went to the clock that chimed, looking at it carefully as if it would attack me. It had been designed to stand freely. The cabinet work was good and the face was kind of interesting. It had easy-to-read numbers but the hands were strangely crooked. I opened the back, noticing the soot and dirt around the escapement. There was a small flashlight tucked away on a small ledge. I took it and used it to check out the rest of the innards. The works were made with brass with very little copper if any — nothing unusual. The clock was very dirty with black, heavy incrustation. It also had oily brass plates, but the bottom had been renovated. There was new wood there that was unusual. I suspected a false bottom. An area in the center of the new wood looked like a key hole. With the flashlight in hand, I checked the pendulum, which was beautiful. Then I looked at the sides of the clock and saw something strange hanging from the right side. Attached to the side there was a dark, worn patch of cloth. I picked it out of its home. It was a pocket of sorts that I unsnapped. There was a shiny gold watch inside. It was a wind-up, white-faced Omega pocket watch with an unusual stem that looked like a key of sorts. At the bottom of its face between the numbers five and seven, there was a small circle containing a second hand. There wasn't a number six on the face of the watch. I had never seen anything like it before. Pleased with this discovery, I knew my decision was made. Then I remembered the hole in the false bottom. Following my instincts, I placed the stem of the watch into the hole. It was a perfect fit and I heard a snap. I opened the false bottom without a hitch and there I found a treasure. Money. Loads of money!

I stood up so fast I almost got dizzy. My head spun around to see if Jimmy the Mope was watching me. If he was he must have been an invisible man. There was no one around. I was completely alone. I had to act fast before Jimmy returned. I hunched up back into my kneeling position and looked at the three bundles. Each stack had a hundred dollar bill on top. My head started to spin. Should I take one out and show it to my father? Should I leave the stacks where they were and return everything back to its original? Should I just take the watch? Maybe my father hid the money. Maybe he was stealing from Stan. Then I thought about Stan. Was it his money? It couldn't have been my father's because he let me have the run of the place. If there was any chance of me finding it he wouldn't let me search around like this. Then I knew I couldn't take the money or the bag out because Jimmy would see me with it.

Better not take a chance on anyone seeing it. Jimmy could show up at any minute. Hundred dollar bills carefully stacked and hidden. . . and I found out about it. . . what luck. On my birthday, no less. Pleased with my decision, I decided to return everything back to where it was. But I kept the pocket watch with its pouch. In a

A Birthday

desk nearby I found a small pocket knife. I cut my initials into the desk so I could find it again. With the watch in my hand I retraced my steps to the area by the trap door with a smile on my lips. I called Jimmy's name and he answered by appearing from behind the staircase. I found him with a finger over his mouth to signify we must be quiet. I kept my mouth shut.

When we returned to my father, he was talking to his friend Dutch. They were arguing about something, but changed the subject as soon as they saw us. Dutch was usually a quiet guy, except when he had a few drinks. He could get pretty nasty and Dutch and my father had a history of fights. Dutch moved furniture for Stingo Movers so he was a big guy yet he had a sensitive side to him. He was a serious artist and loved to paint in his spare time.

"So Dutch, how's my older son Frank doing? Does he have any talent?" my father asked.

"Listen Pat, you have to give him some time. Rome wasn't built overnight you know."

"Well, I just want to know that I appreciated the way you found him a studio in the Village."

"What can I tell you? I got good friends. Dino my Greek friend found the place."

"What do you say, let's go over to Murphy's and I'll buy you a drink. Hey son, did you find anything?"

"Sure, Dad. I found a beauty of a pocket watch."

"Well, you'll have to show it to everyone when we get to Murphy's. I've got a thirst that can't wait."

Dutch with his piercing eyes asked Jimmy if he wanted to join them.

"Hey, thanks, Dutch. I'm thirsty, too, but I've got to stick around here and earn my pennies while I can."

"Come on Pat. Give him a coffee break so he can have a beer."

"You know the rules, Dutch, no drinking on the job."

"Hey, I always drink on the job. How do you think I got these muscles?"

"All the muscles went to your head. It's a miracle Stingo didn't catch you when you misplaced those two chairs last week."

"Let's not talk about that. Hey Johnny, I heard you were gonna have your first real beer today."

As usual my father didn't give me a chance to reply, "Not only that. By picking out a watch on his twelfth birthday, he becomes part of the best union around, the watchmaker's union. The watch is his symbol or badge... he's going to be one of "The Guardians."

"Congratulations, kid."

On the way to Murphy's, I thought about how I had watched my father drink beer for a long time and now I was going to find out why he liked it so much. When I asked to try it in the past, my mom always refused and my dad agreed with her. Finally, for my birthday she went along with the idea. I was going to have a beer.

Murphy's Pub was one of my favorite places in the neighborhood. It was a typical Irish pub and it was located right at the corner of our block. About once a week my father would take us there for a family meal where we would eat shepherd's pie, corned beef and cabbage, or chicken pot pie — my favorite. I was only allowed to drink soda at these get-togethers. But now I was a man. This place had a real history in our family. Newly divorced, my father proposed to my mother here. I was convinced that after celebrating at Murphy's one summer night I was conceived. The twinkle in my father's eye engendered my presence into the world. My father was convinced that his singing was the cause of my mother's passion. She claimed it was the shepherd's pie.

Paintings of Ireland, especially of Sligo in the west, were featured throughout the establishment and added to its charm. One of my older brothers, Frank, who wanted to become a painter, had as his goal to have one of his paintings hung here. Small statues of leprechauns guarded the corners of the room. Longshoremen, carpenters, plumbers, accountants — all dreamers — shared stools and tables under faded pictures of W.B. Yeats and James Joyce.

Stingo, another one of my father's friends, yelled out when we

A Birthday

saw him, "Hail, to the Kellys." He came over and slapped me on the back almost tripping and spilling his beer over me, "To what do we owe this honor, Johnny?"

"Well, my father says that I'm a man today. It's my birthday."

Stingo shook my hand and bowed to me, "Well, this calls for a celebration. Let's get a table."

Mousey, Tiny, and Stan joined them and my father enjoyed flaunting his generosity in public by insisting that he treat everyone.

"How old is the youngster?" Stan asked, inspecting me out of the corner of his eye.

"He's twelve, going on twenty," my father laughed.

"I bet he's got the smarts of his mother," Mousey offered.

"Thank God he's not like you," Stingo quipped, flashing a sly smile.

"I'll second that," said Dutch pushing my father's arm.

Not to be outdone, Mousey decided to ask my father a question that I was not happy to hear, "Have you told him about the bees and the birds yet?"

Stingo let out a roar, "It's not the bees and the birds, but the birds and bees. You never get anything right, Mousey."

"What's the difference? I did okay. I got two kids, don't I?"

"What's he talking about?" I asked.

"I guess you told him about the stork, right Pat?" Stingo offered.

"The stork? Come on, Stingo. . . that story is from the Middle Ages."

I couldn't take any more of this stuff, "Dad, I know a lot more than you think."

Then my father had another one of his brilliant ideas, "Listen, guys, I want you each to give my son a one-sentence input as advice in this matter. How about you, Dutch? Do you want to be first?"

Just then the waitress came by with the drink order. "Saved by the drink," Dutch laughed. "Actually, it gives me more time to think."

Stingo chimed in, "You need more than time. But anyway, let's drink to Johnny's birthday."

All the glasses were clinked. The beer was not like I thought it would be. I didn't like it. How the hell was I going to drink the whole glass? Dutch saved me from another taste, "Whatever you do Johnny, don't marry an Irish girl with red hair. They've got a hot temper."

My father agreed. "Remember that, son. I've had some experience in that field."

Everyone enjoyed a good laugh at that comment so my father continued, "Well, that wasn't exactly what I expected from you, Dutch. We have to be more explicit here. Stingo, take a stab at it."

"Hey son, take precautions. You know, when it rains you have to protect yourself. You have to use something like an umbrella. I'll explain further. . . later on."

There was more laughter. "You might want to take notes, Johnny," Tiny offered.

My father tried again, "Be more specific guys. Mousey?"

"Make sure she doesn't talk too much. That's specific."

Tiny had some pretzels in his mouth when it was his turn to speak, but that didn't bother him. He always talked with food in his mouth. "I learned everything about sex from a great book: The Karma Sutra. I have an extra copy that you can borrow."

"Does it have any pictures?" Mousey wanted to know.

"What's the name?" I wanted to know.

"Let's move on," my father said with that weary look in his eyes.

It was Stan's turn. "Now I've been married four times. I know everything about women. I know how they tick. If you have any questions you can always come to me."

I was so frustrated with all this advice that I just had to blurt out, "So what does all this have to do with the birds and bees?" I picked up my pint and forced myself to take a manly drink of beer. I still didn't like it.

My father finally answered my question, "Your mother will explain."

Stan started to prepare his cigar, "Your father told me you were going to pick out something from the store. Did you find an expensive watch?"

I didn't want to show him the watch. I only wanted my father to see it but my father insisted, "Go ahead, son, show Stan the watch."

I fished into my pocket and showed him the pouch. As he ran his hands over the pouch, he looked at it suspiciously. He opened the pouch and took out the watch. He took a loupe out of his pocket and examined the face. The rest of the group looked on in silence.

"Very interesting. This old case is in good condition," he murmured in an inscrutable tone. I held out my hand to take back my watch. Slowly, he put the watch back in its pouch. He arched his eyebrows and gave it back to me with an icy smile.

"Where did you find it?"

"It's a secret. . ." I announced knowing my father would approve. Stan frowned and looked at my father.

Stan looked at me with his small beady eyes, "You must have found this in the back room near my desk. I'd like to buy it back from you, Johnny. Because your father is my partner, I'll give you a good price. How about fifty dollars?" He looked at me with a wolfish smile. "What do you say? That's good money for an old watch."

The guys at the table agreed. Stan gave me a triumphant look and pulled out his wallet. Then he counted out two twenties and a ten, "Two Jacksons and a Hamilton."

He gave them to me. The guys oohed and ahhhed.

I shook my head no.

He scowled.

"Don't be greedy, son. I'll give you three Jacksons, my final offer."

I repeated my former action.

He shot a poisonous look at my father.

"Don't look at me," my Dad said. "I'm only his father."

Stan leaned toward me confidentially and for a second I thought he showed me a look of respect that had not been there a moment before.

"We'll make a deal. Tomorrow, Monday in the afternoon, drop by my house. Bring the watch. I'll make you an offer you won't be able to refuse."

"Fine," I agreed. I don't know why I agreed, but I always figured that I could change my mind and not show up.

Meanwhile, the conversation turned to baseball and I was all ears, occasionally yelling out some statistics that surprised Stingo and Dutch. Stan seemed distracted and did not join in the conversation. He remained quiet observing me with a fake smile. I drank my pint of Guinness but I thought it was very bitter and had no idea how they could drink the horrible stuff.

It was time for me to leave, but when I stood up I felt a little woozy. I was swaying a bit. Noticing my condition, my father asked Mousey to make sure I got to the apartment in one piece. My father told me that he had some important things to take care of and that he would be home in an hour or two. Out of the corner of my eye, I could see Stingo and Dutch winking at each other.

Dutch asked my father, "That important business wasn't going to be at Cunningham's Tavern, was it?" Stingo chimed in, "Are you going to make another contribution to Carol again?"

"Well, I have to. It's good for the business."

"Yes, yes. . . ." they agreed. It was good for the business.

Mousey, my Dad, and I left by the side entrance of Murphy's. It was closer to my apartment house on 55th Street. Then Dad left us. Mousey had his arm around me to make sure I wouldn't fall. My thoughts were a bit jumbled from the beer and I felt fine even though I was talking up a storm. At the apartment house I told Mousey that I could make it up the stairs on my own. He wasn't sure, but I almost yelled at him, that I was a man now and could take care of myself. He gave me some chewing gum to cover the

A Birthday

smell of the alcohol. Then I remembered that I hadn't told Dad about the money. I'd have to tell him later, when we were alone.

When I walked into the vestibule, I did fine. Mousey was watching me from the sidewalk. When he left I tried to open the downstairs door with my key but it didn't seem to fit. After about five minutes, I got lucky. Mrs. Olsen was coming outside from apartment 2A and she opened the door for me. When the door closed behind me, I almost lost my balance and at the same time almost swallowed my gum. I could tell that Mrs. Szablinski was cooking cabbage again by the smell coming from the first floor. I hesitated by the stairs and turned around. There was someone in the vestibule trying to enter. I couldn't make out who it was. Maybe it was Stan trying to get the watch from me. I didn't like him. I started going up the stairs quickly. I had to stop and hold on to the banister. Suddenly, I was afraid that I would fall backwards. Although my head was spinning a bit, I tried to look down the steps. I felt that I was going to fall down the stairs. I forced myself to hold on to the banister with both hands. I could have used Mousey's help now. Why did I tell him I didn't need him? I was scared, but I tried to imagine that the fires of hell were below me. Finally, I was able to ascend to the top of the first flight.

Then I heard the buzzer from the vestibule. I was positive that Stan was downstairs. I was on the second floor now and had to get to the fourth. By some kind of miracle (was I praying and not realizing it?), I went up the second flight two steps at a time. I heard Stan coming up slowly but steadily. I was on the third floor but breathing heavily. The absence of light in the hallway made me think that someone was waiting for me on the fourth floor. Maybe it was one of his friends coming from the roof. He could have climbed up the fire escape to the roof, opened the door on the roof and started down the stairs to cut me off from my apartment. One step at a time, I told myself. Stan was catching up to me from behind. My senses were reeling but I continued to climb. Then Stan was behind me. I could taste the danger, so I turned to fight my enemy with my fists.

"What's the matter Johnny?" Mr. Larsen asked flinching.

Relieved I muttered, "Sorry, I thought you were someone else."

"Are you okay? You look a little unsteady."

"I'm fine, Mr. Larsen. I just don't feel that well." That's when I told myself I would never have another drink ever.

My mother opened the door. "I thought I heard your voice, Johnny. Where is your father? Hello, Mr. Larsen. How are you?"

They had a little conversation as I slipped into the apartment.

I couldn't believe that my mother was sending me out to get my father. We had finished dinner without him and everyone in the family was getting ready for my party. Maybe they wanted me to leave so they could do some last minute wrapping of my presents. I was feeling better and was able to take two steps at a time descending towards the vestibule. I started up the street toward Murphy's. Then I remembered the guys saying that Dad was going to Cunningham's. He took me there once but that bar was on 58th Street and 2nd Avenue. It would take me longer to get there. It was cold out so I felt that would help me to move faster. When I got to the bar, I didn't see my father so I asked the barmaid if he had been there. She wanted to know who I was and why I was looking for Patrick Kelly. When I told her she got a hold of Sam to take me up to see Carol. When I knocked at the door, a woman's voice answered. "I told you we were not to be disturbed."

"I have to see my father," I yelled.

"Someone's at the door," I heard her say. "Says he's your son."

"Oh, God, why now? At this time? Which son is it?"

She was laughing. "I'll go in the other room. Hurry up and get rid of him, so we can go back to business as usual."

I could tell by my father's voice that he was annoyed. "Who is it?"

"It's Johnny."

A Birthday

"What the hell are you doing here!" he yelled. Then I could hear him whisper to someone, "Where the hell are my pants?"

Carol was laughing harder. "Where they usually are. On the floor by the bed."

Finally, my father opened the door a bit. He didn't want me to see what was inside.

"Dad, mom sent me for you and I have to tell you that I found money in the clock."

"No more beer for you, do you hear me? That's the last drink you drink with me. What money are you talking about? And what clock?"

The door opened a little more and I could see a woman in a red slip walking across the room to another door. "Stan wants the watch because it opens the false bottom."

"Calm down, son. . . be quiet. We'll talk about this on the way home. Now go downstairs. I'll meet you there in five minutes."

"Are you with Carol, Dad?"

"Yes, but don't tell your mother. Promise me."

More secrets. This was some birthday. Suddenly, I felt very sad. My father noticed. "She's just a friend, son. We were going over some business. Look pal, let's make this a secret between us, between two men. When you grow up, you'll understand about these things." He put his hand on my shoulder, but I shrugged it off.

He whispered, "She's nothing to me, son. I was just feeling lonely."

"Mom's waiting for you," I said loudly so Carol could hear.

I went downstairs and I felt as if I had a burden on my shoulders. I felt old. I just wanted to go home and sleep. Being a man wasn't going to be easy.

The Motel Room

He was looking out the half-opened window into the dark woods. It was a warm night and he could smell the scents of the silent earth. The room was dark, except for the touch of light that was coming from the bathroom. The sheets lay heavy on his naked body while he waited for her. He kicked them off. The light flicked off in the bathroom and the door opened softly. As he watched the darkness of the woods mingle with the darkness of the room, he heard her walking on the bare carpet with her naked feet. He was quiet and still as she slipped by his side. He could smell her perfume and could feel the warmth of her skin touching his. She ran her hand over his chest tenderly and he stirred slightly.

She leaned over and kissed the palm of his hand. He seemed distant, she thought, but maybe she was imagining it. Tonight she would make him happy.

She placed her mouth on his and kissed him long and tenderly. Pleasant tingling sensations flooded him. He knew that she loved him. Her skin was so beautiful, so soft. He noticed she had her eyes closed while she was kissing him. When he first met her and kissed her he had told her that she must be pretending he was someone else. She laughed and called him silly. She told him — it was so much more beautiful if you closed your eyes. The touching of the lips became more inviting.

It's so lovely like this, she reflected, so beautiful to be in his arms.

He kissed her so tenderly, always tenderly. She felt safe and protected. How nice it would be if they could remain like this forever.

She's like a little girl sometimes, he thought. The way she cuddles up to me now makes me feel as if I could protect her from all harm. He gathered her towards him. He whispered her name softly.

He loves me, she thought. I know it in my heart. He loved me the first time we met. He said that wasn't true, but she liked to believe it was love at first sight. A deep soft sigh welled up inside her. Maybe it was the way he whispered her name. She loved it when he was like this.

He had never been with anybody like her.

After they made love, he fell asleep and Tessie thought about how she had prepared for the night. She had stepped out of the shower; then she admired herself in the mirror while she was still wet. She considered herself petit and attractive, with lustrous straight hair and flashing blue eyes. Actually, she didn't like to admit it but she did take after her beautiful Polish mother. With a towel, she began to dry her dark brown hair and let it fall loosely on her shoulders. She wrapped herself in her pink robe and lit a cigarette. Her heart sang and her thoughts were racing. She took a drag and tried to imagine what would happen tonight. She remembered how she first met Dino. Smoke enveloped her eyes when she relived those early morning motorcycle rides they took together. She placed a few rollers in her hair. With the cigarette in her mouth, she finished the job. When the rollers were in place, she took out a bottle of red wine, and poured herself a glass. It was their sixth anniversary together.

She relaxed and sipped her wine. She took one last look around the apartment to make sure it was clean. She loved to walk around the apartment naked. Last time she forgot to pull down the shades but not this time.

The Motel Room

She went back to the bathroom to begin her makeup ritual. Of course, she brought her drink with her. She lined her eyes just the way she liked them. With a pencil of magenta lipstick she outlined the shape of her lips so that when she sipped from her glass of wine she would not smudge it. When Dino kissed her upon entering her apartment he would taste wine and be flooded with memories. She was sure of that. The final piece of the puzzle would be the earrings. Should she pick the big gold hoops or the delicate ones he had bought her? She chose the delicate ones. He would love that. Now all she had to do was get dressed and rehearse her little speech to him.

She returned to the mirror and started talking, making faces and appropriate gestures, "Look Dino, I'm 23 and I'm not getting any younger and I've got to get away from my mother who's driving me crazy and from my boring job at that printing company. Let's run away together. We could live in a big white house with a picket fence and I can just see it now: our dog running down the hill to greet us when we returned from work. We could move to Las Vegas and work for the casinos. I hear that they send you to a gambling school and you and I could make good money there and we could work together, me shuffling cards and spinning the roulette wheel and you at the blackjack table. I just know we would have a great time."

She had known him in the neighborhood since she was thirteen and had a crush on him. Finally, after four years of waiting, he had asked her out on a date. So that means they had been going out for six years and nothing was happening. He was always talking about getting a decent job instead of working in his father's diner. But he had little ambition and on top of that he liked to gamble. He was forever playing the lottery or the numbers or betting on the baseball and football games. He was even betting on soccer. "Don't you want to save money so you can buy a house like your parents?" she would ask him and he would reply, "I don't think so. I just want to enjoy life and ride my motorcycle with you." Then she found out when he was a kid that he wanted to become an airline pilot. "Well, why don't you become one now by going to school?" she suggested. "I was never good at school," he replied. "Then," she smiled, "I could help you study. That would be fun." "We'll see," he said, giving her his stock answer. She thought Dino was spoiled. He was the only child and his parents gave him everything he wanted except they didn't want him to be a pilot because they thought it was dangerous and he would be flying all around the world instead of living near them. So he did nothing. After a while, he just changed. He became depressed. He didn't want to go to parties like he used to, and for a while he ignored her.

That's when she thought their relationship was over for good. She started to see Frank, who was her boss at the printing company. He said that he was divorced and his wife and daughter hated him. Frank would marry Tessie — in a nanosecond. He said that he was crazy about her. He promised that he would take care of her and love her for the rest of her life and he would take her to Poland. He would buy her whatever she wanted. He even went to see her mother and told her how much he loved Tessie. Frank's parents were Polish and her mother knew his mother. Before Tessie knew it her mother wanted her to give up Dino and give Frank a chance. The problem was that Tessie didn't care for Frank all that much. It was Dino she loved. Frank was ready to get an apartment for her in Manhattan and pay her rent and furnish the place too. He was a decent-looking guy who dressed well, not like the other stiffs at Reed and Quill Press. One of the things she did not like about Frank was that he was so controlling. He always wanted to know where she was going and with whom. Sometimes she felt as if he was stalking her. She felt that someone had been going through her personal belongings at work and she always felt uneasy when walking home alone, as if she were being watched. She found him following her one day and she told him off. That's when Dino looked as if he would get his act together. Dino suddenly started winning lots of money at the track with his system and with tips from an ex-cop he knew. He also got lucky with his bets on the Jets, Giants, and Rangers. He called her. He started spending all his money on her, buying her pretty jewelry and taking her out to dinner. Then he started talking about getting engaged. He would get a real job. She still loved Dino so much. She knew he loved her, truly loved her. Then Dino hit some rough spots. Lady Luck turned her back on him and he started borrowing money. He was lucky enough to get a job at a gas station.

Christmas had just passed without an engagement ring. If she did not get her engagement ring tonight on their anniversary, that would be the last straw. That would be it. She would leave Brooklyn. She would say adios to Dino, and hope that Frank would disappear somehow. She would leave for Las Vegas where she had friends. Leaving Dino would not be easy.

She took another drink and looked into the mirror and started to cry. She said out loud to the mirror, "I love you, Dino, but we can't make it." She started thinking about the good times they had together. He had this powerful shiny motorcycle that he loved and after midnight they would usually find some deserted roads and he would race and turn corners quickly and he would drive recklessly and take her breath away. He was wild on those rides and she would hang on to him for dear life. Then around two in the morning he would find a deserted park and they would make love under the stars. She could feel the cool grass, the air, his lips... but it was winter now. Thinking about this made her cry even more.

The phone rang. Perhaps it was Frank. It made her nervous. Maybe it was Dino telling her that he would be late. She picked it up on the third ring. Then she heard the cold, tiny voice of her mother.

"Hi, what's up?"
"Frank called me."
"When?"
"Just now, a little while ago."
"What did he want?"
"I'm not sure."
"Did he ask about me?"

"Of course he did. He was looking for you to take you to some club. He said you didn't answer the phone."

"Oh, Mom, you know I don't want to see him."

"Calm down. Did I disturb you?"

"Of course, you disturbed me. I'm getting ready for my date with Dino. It's our anniversary."

"Is he going to propose?"

"How do I know, Mom. I don't have a crystal ball?" Deep down she thought the ring would never appear.

"It won't help for you to be angry. I'm sorry I mentioned it," her mother offered, guessing her daughter's thoughts.

"Did you tell him where I was going?"

"Of course not. I'm not that stupid, you know."

"I never called you stupid, Mom."

"Yes, but you thought it. Your father always called me that."

"Mom, don't bring that up now."

"Listen, I just wanted to tell you that Frank called, that's all. If anything goes wrong with you and Dino, you can always count on him."

"Is that what he told you to tell me?"

"No, he didn't tell me to say anything to you. Sweetheart, there's no reason for you to be so agitated."

"The point is I don't want to see him anymore. He's a stalker."

"No, he's not dear. At your age you don't know anything about men. He's just lonely, that's all. I understand him."

"Then why don't you go out with him, Mom?"

"Sweetheart, don't be like that."

"Mom, I've got to get ready. Dino will be here at any minute. I'll call you tomorrow."

"Goodbye, dear. Don't worry. Just have a good time."

She was upset. There were no ifs and buts about it. She remembered when her mother called Dino a bum. It was during that time when things were going really bad for him. Tessie defended him but she couldn't say anything when he disappeared for three weeks. Even

Dino's parents didn't know where he was — or at least that's what they said. When he reappeared, he tried to turn it into a joke saying it was a very early midlife crisis. He told her that he drove his motorcycle and pretended he was like that movie star James Dean going from place to place without a destination. When she pressed him for more, he said he had to be alone to fight his demons. No one could help him. He just wanted to be alone.

Tessie looked at the clock. She would have to hurry. She put on her black dress and then pulled the rollers quickly from her hair. She combed her hair back the way her mother used to do it and she thought about how Dino loved her in the black dress — it turned him on. She wanted to give him one beautiful night so he would remember her. Dino was the first man that she was ever with and then there was Frank.

Frank was always persistent in trying to renew her interest in him. She'd meet him from time to time for dinner, because he told her he was having trouble with his daughter Cristina who was twelve. He claimed his ex-wife was poisoning her, that she was badmouthing him. Tessie felt sorry for him and advised him to see Cristina as often as possible. He told Tessie that he took Cristina to lunch and that the lunch didn't go well and Cristina accused him of not caring about her and breaking all his promises. She told him not to give up — everybody needs a father. Frank's relationship with his daughter did get better and he told her that it was because of her.

Frank kept trying to see Tessie after work, creating situations where they would have dinners together. He would continually call her at odd hours and seemed obsessed. In the end it didn't work out well for her. Maybe it was just him or maybe it was her love for Dino.

No, the best way was to quit her job and leave town if Dino didn't propose. That might be the best way.

When she heard the bell, she opened the door, but there was no one there. She closed the door and smiled. Then she heard the bell again.

"Who is it?" she asked.

"It's a delivery," a familiar voice replied.

"What do you have for me today?"

"Looks like a box of chocolates."

"Sorry, not interested."

"Maybe it's a bouquet of flowers."

"No, that won't do either."

"It looks like a hunk of a man."

As she opened the door, Dino handed her a bouquet of flowers and began singing, "You're my everything."

They played this game almost every time he called and she never knew what to expect. She took his flowers, kissed him, and brought him down the long narrow corridor that went past the bathroom and opened up into the living room. Coffee, her cat, came out from under the couch to be admired and stroked. She was a sleek, small creature with beautiful silky fur. Dino took the cat in his arms and she immediately began to purr.

Tessie crept up beside them. "What would you like to drink?"

"Since it's out sixth anniversary, let's break out the champagne, the bottle we've been keeping for a special occasion."

They took the champagne out and he popped the cork. They laughed because the cork almost hit the clock. After the bubbly flowed, they twined their arms around each other and drank to their six years together.

Dino was different tonight. He seemed more affectionate than usual. She liked that. He told her how beautiful she looked in her black dress. "Come closer, Tess. I want to whisper something sweet to you."

"You weren't taking drugs tonight with Nicos... were you?"

"No, my love, but we did have a few beers."

"I don't like him, Dino."

"But, he likes you."

The Motel Room

"I'm not so sure he's good for you."

"Don't worry. Forget about him. It's our anniversary. We are going out for a beautiful dinner and then we are going to the best run-down motel in town — the one we went to six years ago. Come on Tessie. Let's drink to that."

They started to crack up laughing. Then they twined their arms together and drank.

She was looking out the half-opened window in their motel room. It was a warm night and she could smell the scents of the silent earth. The room was dark and soon she would wake him and tell him. Suddenly, the phone rang. It startled her and she didn't know what to do. He woke and answered it without thinking.

"Who?"

She listened. Who could be calling?

"Tessie? You want to talk to Tessie?" he handed her the phone.

Her heart seemed to stop beating. She held her breath. She put the phone to her ear, hoping he didn't see her hand shaking. "It sounds like they hung up," she told him.

Dino turned around to face her, "Who the hell is Frank?"

She reached across his body and hung up the phone on his night table. A sudden wave of anger brought a flush to her face and she blurted out, "How the hell do I know? I can't take this life — we aren't going anywhere. What I want you don't want, and what you want I don't want. Don't you understand? I'm leaving. I'm going to Las Vegas. My girl friend is going to get me a job out there." She began to cry.

There was a long silence. They just sat there looking at each other not knowing what to say. The phone rang again. Music was coming from next door. She saw that he was very angry.

Tessie wanted to leave. She grabbed her clothes and ran to the bathroom. When she returned he told her, "Maybe you should go home."

"Yeah, maybe I will."

He was very quiet. She opened the door, turned around and said, "I still love you, Dino." She closed the door.

Suddenly, he ran to the door completely naked and opened it. He shouted to her, "I don't care if you ever come back. I found somebody else. Who needs you anyway?"

He slammed the door and slowly retreated to the bed. The music was still playing next door and he heard the words, "Don't leave me baby, now, when I need you so."

Johnny Grows Up

Johnny was playing his favorite game, throwing pennies on to the train tracks at the last stop of the R subway line in Brooklyn. He was trying to get one penny to lie flat on one of the two tracks so that the train would pass over it and flatten it. He had to be careful that no one saw him especially his uncle Mike who was a motorman on the R line. Johnny loved this station and always sought refuge here. It was usually cool and dark in the summer and warm and light in the winter. The best part was no one knew he was here. He heard the sound of the train approaching the station and stopped throwing the coins. His uncle might be driving this train and Johnny didn't want his uncle to catch him at his game.

The train pulled into the station with a great deal of noise. He always thought of the trains as giant snakes moving through the tunnels. Big Mike congratulated him on his vivid imagination. "Pretty good for a nine year old," he would always say. Johnny figured he said that to help his memory regarding Johnny's age.

Speak of the devil, here was Big Mike now heading towards the front car. Everybody could recognize Big Mike from far away. He would move confidently on the platform like some redheaded Irish hero except that he was wearing a blue uniform. He was a huge guy, about six-feet-four and weighing over two hundred pounds, a man of action, who always had a big grin on his face.

"Hey, Johnny, you should be getting home now. It's almost dinner." He had no trouble lifting Johnny up in the air. "How's my favorite nephew?" That always made Johnny laugh because he knew he was the only nephew. "Get along now and give a big kiss to your mother Rose for me."

After being let down, Johnny gave him a big salute and started running down the subway platform to the stairs. He had forty blocks to get home and only fifty minutes to make it. He was cutting it close. If he was late again his mother would definitely yell at him. Why couldn't he get her to praise him once in a while? She was always praising his sister, his antsy sister Annette or his brother Frank but never him. She told him his imagination was too wild and his curiosity always got him in trouble.

On the way back home, he was thinking about this unfairness. Annette was the apple of his mother's eye. "She's always been a joy to me. She does well in school and she always helps me around the house." On the other hand when she spoke to Patrick, it was always, "Johnny will be the death of me. He's a thorn in my side. What am I going to do with him? You have to discipline him better, Patrick." Meanwhile, he moved quickly along the streets amid the returning workers from Manhattan. He passed Schultz's butcher shop, John's Deli, Nick's Fruit and Vegetable store, and the Norwegian bakery. He charged up the stairs of his apartment building knowing that he was late again. The smell of the Irish stew made him happy even through he knew he was walking into trouble.

"Oh, finally, the king is here," yelled his mother.

Despite her sarcasm, Johnny could see that his mother was in a good mood, so he slid into his seat at the table and helped himself to the bowl of stew that had been placed in the center of the table. "Now that Johnny is here, I can announce that Annette is going to be playing a lead role in Arthur Miller's play at the neighborhood theater."

"Nice going," Frank replied, smiling at his blond-haired sister.

"Isn't that great, Johnny? Don't be jealous of your sister. Share her joy."

"Yeah, that's great, Ann," he mumbled as he smoldered inwardly, knowing that his sister hated it when he called her Ann instead of Annette.

"Well, let's hope that one day it will be your turn to be a great actor. You certainly have the imagination," his mother offered without confidence.

Frank, sensing Johnny's discomfort, added, "When he tells his stories, I think he shows great acting potential." He winked at Johnny and Johnny smiled in gratitude.

"Now, where is Brian?"

With this question, Johnny watched his mother's face shadow with seriousness. He knew that she was worried about him and the new friends he had made.

"He works hard, Mom," Frank said. "He probably just stopped off for a drink with the guys. He has his troubles. He should be here soon."

"He should be on time. It shows respect. If your father was here, believe me he would be on time."

Johnny thought to himself, My mom is tough. She's a tough lady.

As if he knew they were talking about him, Brian entered the apartment and swung into the kitchen. He greeted his mother with brashness, swinging his right arm around her shoulders and planting a kiss on her cheek. His mother stiffened, but Johnny noticed a trace of amusement around the corners of her mouth. "Is that liquor I smell on your breath?"

"Liquor? No, Ma, just a glass of beer. I just stopped for a quick one."

Rose eyed him carefully. "Never mind your hellos with your friends. You should be on time. You can't get anywhere in this world unless you're punctual."

"What happened at work today?" Annette asked.

Brian started off on one of his long tales and the family settled down. Although Johnny loved Brian's wonderful stories and his charm, it was to Frank that he went to for counsel. With Frank, he felt comfortable and free from the jibes that he got from the rest of the family. After dinner when Frank went to the bathroom to shave for his date, Johnny followed him. It was Johnny's turn to do the dishes, but he told his mother he was soaking the pots, hoping that someone else would finish the dishes while he was with Frank.

After watching Frank shave and look at himself to see his workmanship, Johnny stated, "You know, I'm twice as smart as Annette. I just don't study that much."

"You can say that again. But don't be hard on her. She's a girl and girls are hard to figure out sometimes." He reached over and messed up Johnny's hair.

"Do you understand Cheryl?" Johnny said.

"I'll tell you a secret. . . not a bit."

"Do you love her?"

"Absolutely. Understanding her and loving her are two different things."

"Johnny, what's bothering you?"

"I don't know. It's mom I guess. Why doesn't mom love me, Frank?"

"Listen, kid, you're suffering because you're the youngest in the family, that's all. I'm glad I'm not the youngest. . . it's lonely."

"But why does mom always take it out on me? I didn't hurt her."

"No, you didn't. But remember the time that you pulled Annette's hair? You made her angry but you didn't mean to."

Johnny laughed.

"Sometimes we hurt people without knowing it. Dad and mom are having a rough time these days. And you have dad's looks — you take after him — so, who knows, maybe when she sees you she sees him and she can take it out better on you than him."

"Oh, I see. How did you get so smart Frank?"

"I'm not so smart when it comes to my own life. But read more, Johnny. Read."

Johnny headed back to the kitchen and he noticed that Brian, Annette, and Kathy were gone. He was in purgatory. There was no way of escaping the dishes. Slowly, he began to work. He knew that his mother was watching him as she pretended to darn some socks. In a few minutes, Frank walked into the room dressed for his date. He said good night to his mother, kissed her gently on the cheek, and told her not to wait up for him. Then as he turned toward the door, he paused next to the TV. He waited there a minute. Johnny was watching him with interest. His brother looked thoughtful or troubled.

"Mom, I'd like to talk to you."

"I'll go inside and do my homework," Johnny volunteered, hoping to avoid the dishes.

"Stay where you are, Johnny. There's a job to be done and you have to do it. Don't shirk your duty. Go on, Frank. What did you want to say? You can say it in front of Johnny. There's no one else here. They all ran out on me. Just like your father."

"I want to give Cheryl an engagement ring for Christmas."

"Are you sure, son? I mean have you spoken to her about it? She's spoiled and a bit older than you."

"She's not spoiled, Mom. She works hard helping in the store after school and. . . ." Johnny could see Frank was angry at himself for trying to defend Cheryl against his mother. Meanwhile, his mother kept sewing.

"Cheryl always praises you, Mom. She really likes you," Frank offered. He looked from his mother to Johnny. Johnny began working hard on the dishes, excited that he was an observer of this little tete a tete between his mother and his brother.

"Well, good night, Mother. I'll let you know what Cheryl said tomorrow." He left the room quickly.

"Oh, she's going to break his heart. She'll never accept him. He's just a kid to her."

Johnny could hear the hurt in her words. When he turned around he saw that she stuck the needle into her thumb. He went to her, "Mom, you're hurt."

"Hurry up and finish the dishes. It's a mother's life to get hurt.

I'll be all right." Johnny returned to the dishes, puzzled by his mother's words.

The following morning, everyone found out the terrible news: Cheryl refused Frank. As the days passed by everyone saw his self-confidence wane. He became irritable, hard to talk to and nervous. It was a difficult time for him. It was also a difficult time for Brian. He seemed to be drinking more lately and spending more time with his friends, coming home later and later. Annette was coming home later, too, because of the rehearsals at the playhouse. There were rumors that their father had a roaming eye for the ladies. Johnny noticed that his mother was under a lot of pressure so he decided that he was going to do something outstanding to please her. He was going to reform and win a medal in history at school. He had never been a good student because at his school if you did well you got beat up by the kids. The days that followed his decision saw a deep change in him. He spent less time at the 95th street station. He studied harder and became a good student. The teachers saw the change but said nothing. His family did not notice the change in him because they were concerned with their own survival in the cold city. The medal would be awarded in January. At night before going to sleep, he would dream of his mother's joy and surprise. That image became his inspiration and he continued to work hard at his lessons in history. In fact, his marks in math and science were beginning to go up, too.

The final exam in history was to be given on a Thursday. On that Wednesday night, his father had invited some of his friends to come over to play cards. Johnny loved his father's friends and wanted to hear all the stories about Stingo jumping ship, Dutch getting even with his bookie, and Popeye's escape from jail in Ireland, but he skillfully avoided the kitchen, the laughter, and the drinks. He studied and thought of the medal he would win for his mother. That was his goal.

After the test was over his teacher called him to her office. She told him that he had won the medal in history and it would be given to him at commencement. She told him how proud she was of him.

Johnny Grows Up

She knew how hard he worked to win it. Johnny raced down the stairs outside her office. He jumped over the fire hydrant on the corner of Third Avenue oblivious to the snow falling on this January day. When he approached his building he slowed down. He had rehearsed this scene over and over in his head.

When he got to the apartment on the fourth floor he could hear voices coming from the kitchen. He tried to be casual as he entered the apartment. He could hear his sister laughing and his uncle's voice booming. He welcomed this atmosphere and was happy that Big Mike was here. It would please his mother more when he told her the news. He sauntered into the room and sat down on the chair, letting his books fall to the floor.

"Johnny, have some tea and cupcakes with us," Uncle Mike offered in an exuberant manner. His mother seemed happy to see him. Out of sight, his sister Annette made a face at him. His mother began to pour the tea for him. "And what kind of day did you have today, son? You know Annette was just telling us the good news, that she won a medal for English. Aren't you happy for her? She's such a smart one."

"But mother I have some good news for you, too!" he blurted out.

"That's good, son. Try this donut, Mike. It's filled with jelly."

"I won a medal, too — in history!" His body swelled in pride. Uncle Mike slapped him on the back, "Well done. The boy's a scholar." Annette looked at him in shock while his mother muttered, "Well, the saints be preserved. That's good, Johnny, very good. You've been quiet these days. I was wondering if you were sick or something. You were not yourself. You must have been praying a lot."

Uncle Mike started talking with his mouth full of jelly, "Jesus, Mary and Joseph, you have to tell me what saint you've been praying for, Johnny. If he works for you he might be able to get me a raise at work." They all laughed except for Annette, who still had her mouth open in surprise at the news.

And that was the end of it. His mother began talking to Mike about their relations in Ireland. Johnny grabbed his books from the floor and ran to the bedroom where he flung himself on the bed and buried his face into the pillow. I worked so hard, gave up so many things — for what? I win the medal to make my Mom happy and what do I get? She says, "That's good, Johnny, very good." He felt sad. I'll show her. I'll throw myself off the pier and drown. Then she'll be sorry....

They talked for a long time in the kitchen. He could hear their laughter. Were they laughing at him? He sulked for a long time, and then went to the bathroom so that he could wash his face. He looked at himself in the mirror and then he thought about all the heroes he read about in the history books. He wondered if they had problems with their mothers. Then he realized he was feeling sorry for himself. Another monologue entered his head: Hey, you idiot. Your mother will never be happy with you. She will never praise you like you want. There's nothing you can do. It's like Frank wanting to please Dad. He told me once Dad would never praise him, never say that he was proud of him. Frank accepted it and became his own man. Listen, you worked hard and you made something happen. You should be proud of yourself. You don't need anyone else to say you did well. You know you did well and you accomplished something important....

He ran the monologue over again as he looked at himself in the mirror. He was beginning to feel better about himself. And then he heard the familiar command, "Hey, hurry up in there. You're not the only one in the house!" Of course, it was Annette. He washed his face one more time and then walked out of the bathroom with pride in his step and a smile of confidence in his look. He felt he was like his brother Frank, the old Frank, the one who was going to conquer the world one day. He felt as if he had grown up a bit. He felt like a man.

The Ferry

The evening was cool, as only the end of summer can be cool. He was a gaunt man, pale with red hair, about 50, and he was boarding a ferry to get away from the city. He was tired of feeling cooped up in his room. He was out for the evening seeking fresh air and some rural scenery. There was a preoccupied pensive air about him. He seemed not to notice the other passengers. Walking towards the bow of the boat, the noise of the cars and the talk of the people were washed away with the cleanliness and purity of the sea air. The stars stood out in the dark sky; occasionally he looked at them. Something in the sea seemed to draw him, however. He looked deeply into its blackness. The evening was cool.

The blast from the ferry was startling, but he seemed not to notice it. His body did not flinch, nor his mind. It echoed through him, through the emptiness of his mind, through the blankness of his gaze. The ferry rocked gently, and the wooden slip, which just a few moments ago held it captive, moaned and creaked with its loss. The evening breeze stirred gently against his cheeks bringing a glimmer of life to them. The water was black and it swirled frantically with the ferry's movement. The boat shivered with its cargo and with another blast of sound entered the night. The man continued to stare into the unending mysterious sea.

After a short while he sensed someone standing next to him. The man was tall, young, about thirty and robust, healthy looking but on the heavy side. The redheaded man saw him pull out a cigarette from a full pack. He lit it and as he took in the first drag, he lifted his left hand to offer a cigarette. The redheaded man reached out, took a cigarette and said, "Thanks a lot, buddy, I appreciate that."

"Sure, don't mention it. I always enjoy a good smoke on a night like this."

"Yeah, me too. My name's Eddie, by the way." He took a flask of whiskey out of his pocket and offered it to the young man. "I keep this with me in case it gets cold."

"No thanks, Eddie. I don't drink much and I'd rather not have a drink right now. I'm going home to my family. People around here call me Homer by the way. What brings you out on a night like this?"

"Nothing much. Just trying to get away from all the noise and lights of a big city. Say, where did you get a name like Homer?"

"There's a short version and a long version to that story."

"Well, I'd like to hear the longer version if you don't mind. I've always liked talking to strangers; you can learn a lot. In this city we're running around too fast. People don't talk to each other. Anyway, we've got some time on this ferry, so let's hear about it."

"Okay, since we have some time, I'll give you both versions. My mother and father named their first son Homer. He died and so when I was born they named me Homer. Pretty short, huh? Here's the long story: my father was Greek and his name was Demetrius Kochones. He loved two Greek epic poems, both written by Homer. He wanted his son to become a writer. My mom's favorite painter is Homer Winslow. I believe this is the only thing they ever agreed on in their marriage."

"So I guess everyone asks you how you got named Homer."

"Just about. I never liked the name because in grammar school when the kids saw me they would sing "Home on the range" but substitute Homer for Home. Now my wife and I want a son and you can bet we're not going to name him Homer Junior."

"Oh, so you're a family man?"

The Ferry

"Yes, did you ever get married, Eddie? I don't see a wedding ring on your finger."

"Nope. I met a nice lady once, but it didn't work out. So after that experience I kinda stopped looking to marry."

"So, Eddie, you must have a long term girlfriend or something."

"Naw, I had a few girlfriends, but in my twilight years the older women are married and the younger ones won't even look at me anymore."

"So who do you have that is important to you. I mean a man can't live without love, am I right?"

"I was pretty close to my mom and when she fell and broke her hip I took care of her, but she passed away about a year ago. So I haven't been talking to too many people since then. Freedom is pretty important to me, freedom and privacy. But somehow I seem to be talking a lot to you. I always thought of myself as a loner. I want nothing else, no father, no wife, and no house. I want nothing. When you want something, like a house, then you want something else, like new furniture and then you want more and more. I'm convinced, if you want to be at peace, the very first thing is not to want anything."

"Hey listen, Eddie, everybody needs someone. What about your father?"

"He passed away a long time ago. People die or they leave you, abandon you. You can't trust people; they disappoint you. When my father died, I was really upset."

"I understand how you feel. My dad died a few months ago. So I had my mother move in with us. That way my mother wouldn't get lonely. But my mother is a strange woman. She has he own way of doing things. She's from the old country, you know?"

"My mom was from Ireland, Homer, and you couldn't go into the house without taking some holy water with your fingers and blessing yourself. It must be really nice to have your mother live with you. As you get older sometimes you feel like the world has forgotten you. I remember many years ago gathering with the family for holiday dinners. I used to dread all the arguments between us and all that gossip that went on, but these days I find myself missing those times. I have to admit it. So, was it tough on you, losing your dad?"

"Yeah, we were very close. He was a generous man and a social one. He always had a story for every occasion. When I was a kid, he would take me fishing, hunting, and hiking. He loved the outdoors. Oh, we had our fights, but we would forget them after a few days. There's not a day when I don't think about him."

"What did he do for a living?"

"He was a printer. And of course, that's what I do which is why I'm coming home so late tonight. You know, when I first saw you looking at the sea after we got underway, you reminded me of my father. I could have used his help today at the shop. He probably would have saved me some headaches and a lot of work. He knew how to solve problems. You know my wife, Diana, tends to cook way too much food. If you look at our dinner table you would think it was Thanksgiving everyday at our house. How about you come over and grab a bite? Are you hungry?"

"Thanks! It's been a long time since I've sat down and had a good home cooked meal. That would put a smile on my face."

It was a strange-looking house, built far back from the sidewalk, not following the pattern of the row houses to the left and right. It slanted a little under the heavy grape vines that covered the roof and fell along the sides. It was as if the house were trying to hide itself from the world. A woman stood in the door, waiting for them.

Eddie stopped because his heart was starting to behave strangely.

"What's the matter? Are you all right?" asked Homer.

Eddie's heart was beating in different rhythms and he had trouble focusing. A worried look came over his face.

"Just give me a minute. I'll be all right."

The Ferry

They stood there for a short period of time, as if caught in a still picture.

Homer stood by Eddie's side with a concerned look, but didn't utter a word. The woman at the door did not move, but was looking at them intently with patience.

Finally, they began moving toward her. "I'm fine now," Eddie said.

As the woman stood there, he saw at once that she was old like him. She was holding a lighted candle of some kind in front of her and there was a dark passage behind her. She was dressed in a flowing garment that women wore in ancient Greece. She had a regal bearing and yet in all her gestures she expressed a warm welcome towards him, as if she were expecting his visit.

"Well, who is this gentleman, Homer?"

"Met this fine man on the ferry. His name is Eddie."

"Welcome to our home. My name is Athena, Eddie. You'll have to excuse us. We're having some kind of trouble with the lights. Homer, you'll have to find out what's gone wrong."

"I'll get right to it. Is Diana around?"

"She went next door to help our neighbor Mrs. Diaz who had a fall, but she should be back soon. Dinner will be delayed, I'm afraid."

"I'll see what I can do," Homer said as he left the house.

Eddie noticed that Athena was a rather tall woman with a weather-beaten face. Her large dark eyes were penetrating and held his. She seemed to recognize who he was.

Inside, the darkness of the house touched him, as if it were a healing hand. The long hallway led them to the kitchen. The irregular beating of his heart was stilled. The woman set the candle on a kitchen table and Homer told him he had to go in the back and would return soon. She pointed to a chair by the kitchen table. Because of the walk from the ferry, he was hungry and tired, but he was glad that he was in the company of this young man and his mother.

At first he felt secure. His heart was quiet and the room smelled warm and inviting. Someone had been cooking something good. He could see the other room from the kitchen. A bed was made across the passage. The bed had been made up with a dark blue quilt. Eddie did not know how to react to the woman, and all these unfamiliar things that were surrounding him. He had lived the past month in which nothing much had happened to change his routine except for a kind of malaise that kept his spirits down. Heartbeats, dreams, a perpetual kind of fever, and now this. There was a silence in this house, no radio, and no television was on to distract him. Why didn't she say something?

Eddie blurted out, "It's nice to be here."

"My son is a good man. He's a man of many turns. Has he told you about his stories and himself?"

"No, he just told me about the printing company and about your husband."

"I miss him. His name was Demetrius. We were married for forty years but he had to take the journey that we all have to go on."

Eddie wanted to hear more about her, but he was interrupted by her sudden announcement, "Homer will be here any minute now."

She was right. Homer came plunging into the kitchen with a huge dog. The dog strained on the leash to get to Eddie. Eddie quickly moved away from the dog. He didn't like animals. A dog had bit him when he was a kid.

"Don't worry. He don't bite. He just barks a lot — all bark and no bite — like a lot of people," Homer said, smiling.

The dog approached Eddie anyway, barking and sniffing. Eddie gave a false smile but his heart was beating against his ribs. Someone who knew dogs well told him to lick saliva on his palm and let the dog sniff it. That would calm the dog down. He did so and it worked.

"Lights will be on soon," Homer continued. "My brother down the street is fixing the problem. Where's the coffee? Eddie is going to join us for dinner but I think coffee would be good now. Athena's coffee is the best. It will cure what ails you. Ain't that right?"

"You're right, son. I make it the old fashioned way."

The Ferry

"Diana will be over soon. I'll just take King here for a walk. Be right back, Eddie."

Eddie watched the old woman walk over to the stove and put the water on to boil. Slowly, she did everything, slowly. She washed the cups and saucers, placing them on the kitchen table. Athena treated each cup and saucer carefully as if they were fragile and might break. Every task that she performed, she did gracefully. There was kindness and joy in her face. She began singing some kind of hymn. In wonder and awe he felt as if he were in another world. His eyes watched her hands move as if they bestowed a special meaning to everything she touched. He was wrapped up in all her actions.

He suddenly wanted to talk to her, to tell her everything about the way he felt. "You know this past month has been upsetting for me. I've been having trouble sleeping, having bad dreams, seems like I'm not myself anymore. I feel disconnected, out of sorts. Nothing is going right. . ."

He realized she wasn't listening. She was still singing but this time under her breath and she was not paying any attention to him at all. He stopped and said nothing. As soon as he did this, he began to feel emotional. He stared at the woman's back as this feeling got stronger.

He placed a trembling hand over his forehead and looked at the placid woman. He was amazed that she could just by her simple words and mere presence, communicate compassion, something which seemed to escape him. The coffee was ready. She brought the milk and the sugar. He watched her pour the rich dark liquid into his cup. He felt she had entered from another world, maybe another time or perhaps this had all happened before maybe in another life. He found himself praising the coffee after he had tasted its unusual sweetness and the way she had made it. Perhaps there was some old secret beaten vessel where she had prepared this potion. She stood by his elbow and asked if he wanted milk and sugar. He had wanted the coffee black just the way he had always taken it, but some impulse moved him to do something different. "Just milk," he had answered. Again, she poured the rich white milk with her strong fingers commenting on its freshness. Bowing her head, she told him her coffee had always made people happy. That's because she added a secret ingredient.

    He drank the coffee at her bidding and praised it again. And in doing so, he knew that he had praised her also. She smiled and returned to the sink. In that short bit of time, he felt a chill in the air. When he had finished his coffee, however, he felt content. He should have gotten up and walked around a bit, but he didn't want to do anything to ruin this new emotion he had. His heart was full and he wasn't worried about anything at all. The drink was a very strong brew but it made him drowsy. He felt as if he could fall asleep. A strange sound forced him to wake.

    "What's that noise," he asked.

    "That's the stream out back," she said, standing by the table.

    "That's strange. I didn't hear it before."

    She moved to the window by the sink and pointed into the darkness and then a step shook the house and Homer was back without King this time. Eddie became aware of how the woman left him and went to her son's side.

    "I'm sorry about the lights not being on and the dinner not being ready. Everything seemed to happen at once. I guess it was a bad time to invite you to a meal. We'll have to give you a rain check. Listen, I'd like to drive you home — the car is outside. And we should leave soon since it's getting late. I can drive you right to your apartment."

    Eddie wanted to remain here forever, and Homer must have felt that he wanted to stay. "If you want to stay over we could fix up a sandwich for you and you could spend the night with us. My wife will be here in about an hour. Would you like to stay and meet her?"

    "I'm so sorry, but I really have to get back. I need to be heading back. I got some pills I got to take back home. I appreciate the hospitality."

    "If you ever find yourself coming this way again, please feel free to stop by."

The Ferry

"Thanks, I think I will be stopping by again, soon."

"All right, so I'll go get the car started."

"To be honest, Homer, I think I'd prefer to take the ferry back. The sea air will do me some good."

"Are you sure? Are you feeling all right?"

"Yes, I have to get back. Thank you both for your kindness and warmth."

"Think nothing of it. We're happy to know you."

"Wait, I have some Greek cookies for you to take on the ferry," Athena said.

He left the house with Homer at his side and with a final farewell, he headed for the ferry. He knew that he would have to hurry to make the last ferry of the night. The mere idea of rushing made his heart beat faster. When he finally saw the lights and the people boarding the boat, he was sad he was leaving this place.

When he boarded instead of going to the bow of the ferry, he stayed at the stern. He looked at the island and thought he saw the old woman. He took out the bag of cookies and removed one. He raised it in his hand and called out, "To Athena!" His hunger made him devour all seven cookies. She would have liked that, he thought. The blast from the ferry didn't startle him — he had been expecting it. The engines started up and the boat shivered in the water. Soon it was cutting into the water like a knife parting bread. He watched the outline of the shore and its lights receding into the darkness. Something inside him seemed to move in harmony with the water. Before he knew it, the ferry was entering into the open arms of the slip. The wooded greased piles turned the black water into a dirty grey, as the ferry docked. The evening breeze felt good to him, as he stared into the lights.

The people started to file out. He was the last one to leave.

Carmen

Carmen listened to the rain outside her window. Tonight she would get her revenge, and yet somehow the thought depressed her a little. Except for a few candles, her apartment was dark, just the way she liked it. She was playing her favorite tango, "Sabor a Buenos Aires." The light from the candles created mesmerizing patterns on the wall. Maybe she should smoke a joint to slow herself down. She often walked around her living room half-naked, but tonight she was cold. She put on a long red wool sweater over a pair of black tights. She would have a glass of wine instead of a joint, after all.

She opened the bottle and poured herself a glass. Her mother loved to have wine with dinner. How she missed her. Sharing that apartment with her all those years, in that huge tenement on Third Avenue, the Fox Building in Brooklyn, created a special bond. It was there at the Fox Building when she turned fifteen that men had started to notice her. She enjoyed the attention. Her mother watched her carefully, and tried to protect her from the gang members with tattoos crawling on their arms waiting for her to enter the building. She warned her about the bars, sex, smoking marijuana, drinking, drugs, and everything else she could think of. When she was a young seventeen, she met Angelo Motta at a high school function. He was an important man in the community who had connections with the local Chamber of Commerce and several community clubs. He donated money to the school, sponsored trips, and knew the teachers and counselors. He had sought her out and spoke to her for a long time. At the time Angelo was in his forties. Her mother encouraged their relationship, because she believed Angelo could help Carmen, maybe get her a good job. When her mother suddenly died a year later, Angelo had found a place for her to live, a two-family house on 84th Street in a middle-class neighborhood. She remembered how much she had missed her mother. How alone she felt and how kind Angelo had been to her. She had been lucky to have him around. He had been like a father to her. The only thing her real father had ever given her was her last name, Rodriguez; then he had disappeared. Carmen was alone now, but she had Angelo to take care of her.

She took a long sip of her wine, savoring its taste and went into the bedroom. She sat in front of her vanity across from her king-size bed and flipped the switch for the Hollywood lights surrounding her mirror. "Am I beautiful, or what?" she said to herself. She did look stunning. Angelo had told her that he was attracted to the sadness in her eyes and the hint of heartache in her voice. He had told her that she was both bold and vulnerable and that was the magic potion that captured all men's hearts.

Carmen finished her wine. Tonight she would put on her Egyptian eyes and, of course, her fiery red lipstick. The dusty gold eye shadow she had bought on Saturday would highlight her eyes perfectly. With stunning irises, her dark eyes were large, moist, and almond-shaped. For added drama she would wear her hair down and pin the sides with the tortoise-shell clips she had bought in Puerto Rico.

She had it all figured out last night after Angelo left her apartment to go home to his wife and daughter. Stan was the real love of her life. He lived with his family on the same block as she did. As kids they grew up together, and she always thought they would marry. During their teens, they drifted apart and then he found Marie. They still saw each other, but Marie became more important to him. The image of Stan and Marie at the wedding a week ago had really gotten to her. She shouldn't have gone to that damn wedding. She was jealous and was furious at him for the way he treated her at the church and reception. He told her that he couldn't see her anymore. His words cut her and wounded her ego. She had to punish him, to hurt him the way he hurt her.

The idea had come to her suddenly. Johnny was the key. It had come to her with such force and insight that she yelled out his name, Johnny. It had to be Stan's best friend. She would throw a wrench into Stan and Johnny's friendship by seducing him. He was the only one who mattered to Stan. They had all known each other from childhood. Stan had always protected Johnny and Johnny had always been his faithful friend.

That evening she had called Johnny to put her plan into action. Men are so damned stupid she thought. All you had to do was play up to their ego, their vanity. Johnny was an artist. He was so proud of his ability to draw and to paint. Stan said he had talent. She would wait and see. Carmen looked back into the mirror, her head thrown back and a smile on her face. She had asked him to sketch her so she could give the sketch to Angelo as a birthday gift.

She needed another drink. The bell startled her. She quickly dabbed on her favorite perfume and got up from the vanity. As she approached her intercom to let him in, she was glad she had told the owner of the house, Mrs. Maggio, to change her bell. Instead of being harsh and grating, it chimed. She pressed the intercom button with her newly polished red nails. By the time she opened the door, Johnny was already at the top of the stairs. Angelo would have taken longer. Johnny looked taller and thinner than she remembered from the wedding. His brown curly hair was messed up from the wind and rain. He was smiling at her and carrying his sketch pad covered in plastic.

"You're soaking wet!" Carmen exclaimed.

"And you look beautiful," he replied.

She was pleased. "In this old thing? Come on in. Do you want to get out of those wet clothes or do you want a nice stiff drink, or both?"

"A drink sounds great."

"A beer?"

"Whiskey would be fine if you have it."

"If whiskey makes you frisky, I'll give you some. I seem to remember that you take it on the rocks."

He gave her a quick nod of the head, "Say, what's with the candles? I'm gonna need some good lighting if you want me to do your portrait. Candles won't do."

"Okay, okay, I just thought we needed a little atmosphere."

"You are something else, Carmen."

She poured him his drink, but resisted putting on the overhead lights which she hated. "How did you get here?"

"I walked."

"All the way from Fifty-Fifth Street?"

"I love to walk."

"No wonder you're soaked. I do have some dry things if you want to change."

"I might feel a little uncomfortable in your clothes, Carmen, and besides, I'm not that wet," he said, laughing.

Stan would have looked for any excuse to get out of his clothes, she thought. She sighed and handed Johnny his drink. She had left a plate of crackers with cheese on the table. "Try these crackers. I bought them yesterday so they're fresh. What shall I wear, Johnny?"

"What you have on is fine."

"Oh, this outfit will never do. This portrait is for a good friend. Now, you know I can only give you $25 for it."

"It's free, Carmen. This whiskey can be payment."

He took a long swallow. She could tell that he was slightly uncomfortable. She would have to go slowly. Prolonging this might make it more fun.

Then she remembered her Tarot cards. She would have to do the cards.

"Johnny, before you sketch me, I gotta read your fortune first."

"Okay, I guess. Stan told me you were big on cards."

Carmen

Carmen got her cards and poured herself another glass of wine, her third glass.

"Let's not talk about Stan tonight. Is that all right with you? Let's just read your cards." A hint of anger crept into her voice.

"Are you getting upset?"

"Maybe I just didn't want to hear his name tonight. Did it ever occur to you?" Carmen had a quick temper. She was aware of that but this flash of anger surprised her. It jolted her.

She didn't say anything else for awhile and then she asked him to cut the cards. Since the wedding, every time she thought about Stan she got angry. But she was always able to control it. At the wedding he showed her no respect. She cornered him and told him that she still wanted him. He excused himself to go to the bathroom.

Slowly, she placed the cards on the table face up. She didn't like what she saw. Stan's card was there. He would always be around, but not in the way she wanted. She gathered up the cards furiously and held them tightly in her hands and whispered, "Stan."

"What about Stan?" Johnny asked. "Do you see problems for him?"

"I told you I didn't want to talk about him tonight."

"Didn't I just hear you mention his name?"

She got up and turned on the overhead lights. The lights were so harsh that they stared at each other in surprise. To change the mood she took off the tango music and put on the Supremes.

"Look, Johnny, let's forget about the cards." She put them back on the table. "Somehow I don't think it's going to work. The reading isn't favorable."

"Why don't I start drawing you," Johnny suggested.

"I don't like what I'm wearing," she told him. "Relax, have another drink and I'll be right back."

When she entered her bedroom, she thought that this evening wasn't going to work out the way she had planned. She might as well leave the overhead on for her portrait and maybe salvage something. The next step was to choose something to wear. As soon as she opened her closet she knew what would be perfect. She would wear a bright red satin slip with a white quilted satin bed jacket over it. She took a long time to calm herself down and get ready.

When she re-entered the living room, he was finishing his drink. He almost choked on it, so she was sure her outfit had the right effect. The slip revealed just enough cleavage and she knew her long and shapely legs were accentuated by her stiletto heels. She knew what she had and wasn't afraid to show it.

"Whadya think Johnny, do I look all right?"

"Well, Carmen honey, you're certainly pleasing to the eye."

"Do you want me to sit or stand?"

"Looking at those shoes, I think you'd better sit. Why don't you come over here and sit by me first. I want to show you some of my work. Perhaps these sketches will give you an idea of how you'll turn out. I drew some of the girls at the Honey Pot. And if you like them, they're yours."

Sitting next to him on the couch, Carmen decided to get rid of her shoes. She was very close to him and she opened the portfolio so that a portion was on his lap and hers, so that they could look at his work together. In a graceful movement Carmen positioned her left hand, which was supporting the portfolio, so that the back of her hand rested on his thighs. Leafing through the pages, Carmen stopped when she saw a drawing of Mona, who worked with her as a go-go dancer at the Honey Pot. It caught her attention.

"That's my favorite," he said. "It's one of the girls caught off guard, looking lonely and sad at the bar on a slow night."

"That's Mona. You really caught her expression."

She looked at the last picture of Ginger, bare breasted.

"Do you want me to pose like this?" she asked.

He blushed. She smiled with amusement and returned to the first sketch so that he could recover. She was delighted that he had shared these sketches with her. Stan was right. She thought Johnny had talent, but that he was a little naive.

"Are you really going to give me these sketches? As a gift?"

"Do you like them?"

"Yes," she said very quietly, strangely moved. "Everyone gives me flowers, or perfumes, or chocolates, but nothing like this." She leaned over and kissed him on the cheek. His skin was very smooth and warm. There was a scent of lemon on him. "Perhaps, you could teach me how to draw," she whispered in her sultry voice. "You could be my private tutor."

She stood up in front of him and let the white bed jacket slide off her shoulders, "How do you want me, Johnny?"

He was struggling.

"Perhaps, on that chair," he suggested gently.

She walked to the chair and let the straps of her slip fall away, exposing not only her shoulders but also part of her breasts. She could almost hear him sigh. Maybe it would work out after all, she thought. She would try one more time. She got up and changed the music back to the tango. She refilled his empty glass. She turned the overhead light off. Carmen was humming the melody of the tango that was playing. She sang the lyrics to him:

"*En este mundo nada es verdad ni mentira. . .* "

"Que pasa, Carmen?" he responded.

She laughed, throwing her head back. "I love those words: *en este mundo*." She turned around, showing off the curvature of her back and her long black hair. Slowly, she lifted the bottom of her slip. She swayed and moved, using her body to beckon him forward. She untied her hair and shook it free. She was naked now. She took his hand and he followed her into the bedroom. The candles were lit everywhere. In a quick movement, which left nothing to the imagination, she slid under the covers. Then she leaned across the bed toward him to turn off the lamp.

He quickly stripped to his shorts and slipped in beside her. She had turned her back to him so he put one arm around her waist. He whispered her name. She could feel his warm breath and his warm body. She turned to face him and kissed him lightly on the lips. Before he had time to do anything else, she turned on her back and lay staring at the dark of the ceiling. She was thinking about Stan and suddenly felt very sad. Johnny looked at her and noticed a change of mood. She was unhappy. It moved him so he slowly and tenderly caressed her cheek with his fingers. She did not react and he backed off a bit.

"Why are you unhappy?" he asked her.

"Because I don't feel that what I am doing is right."

"Tell me," he said softly.

"Maybe we shouldn't be here tonight."

"Yeah, I'm feeling a little like that myself."

"I don't like what I've become."

"Carmen, you're beautiful."

"I feel so alone."

"Me too, but that doesn't have to be bad. Sometimes we have to be alone to figure things out."

"I want to love someone who loves me and who stays with me. Someone who doesn't leave me."

"Life is leaving and arriving, coming and going. Everything changes —"

"There are ghosts in this apartment, Johnny. The ghosts of my mother and my missing father are here. Both of them and now Stan."

"Stan will always love you Carmen. How could he not?"

"What good is that — he's not here, he's married now." There was an underlying anger in her voice.

They were silent for a while.

"I have something to tell you, Carmen," he said.

She turned towards him suddenly interested. "What is it, Johnny?"

"I've always been in love with you."

"I don't understand, Johnny."

"It's hard to explain. Did you ever see a movie called *The Key*? It's about a man who falls in love with his best friend's girl."

"So, you were in love with me when I was with Stan?"

Carmen

"Yep. Stan knew. Stan will always love you, Carmen. I'm his best friend and he wants me to look out for you."

Carmen raised herself on her elbow and stared at Johnny. "You mean to say Stan is okay with you sleeping here!"

"Yes!"

It was as if a volcano erupted. Johnny was pushed out of the bed with enormous energy. Carmen jumped out of bed. She pushed him several times and he almost got burned by the candles. Johnny rushed to get his clothes on. Again she was pushing him and he almost tripped over her slippers landing on her divan. She glared at him as he made his getaway.

Carmen was furious. There was no revenge for her tonight.

The Visit

Red Kelly walked along Second Avenue, passed the Korean fruit and vegetable store, passed the halal butcher, passed Smitty's candy store, and finally reached the brownstone house. The last time that he stood there was at Christmas, almost seven months ago, and he had been drunk. He didn't remember much of what happened and never found out how he got home. Red took a swig from his flask of whiskey, which he always had on him for courage. Someone told him he had a big fight with his son Jim.

As soon as he rang the bell, he knew he was asking for trouble. He waited. Nobody answered. He felt better. Maybe his son wasn't home. He would try one more time and then he would leave. Just as he was going to ring the bell again, the door opened. It was Mrs. Murphy. Then he remembered what a fool he made of himself that day. He had tried to seduce this woman on Christmas! Either the touch of liquor or the scene of the crime or the woman herself must have brought back the reality of the situation.

Mrs. Murphy, an older woman, smiled at him coquettishly. "Oh, Mr. Kelly, how wonderful to see you again. I wondered where my leprechaun had gone to. Have you come to visit me?"

He looked at her hair with a side-long glance. Was it really blue, he wondered.

"Even if my son wasn't living here, I'd think of excuses to come and see you, Mrs. Murphy." He smiled. He loved sharing his sweet words with the ladies.

"As gallant as ever," Mrs. Murphy said, smiling. "Always looking at the world with rose-colored glasses. Why, I must look like a mess right now. Do I?"

"Nonsense, you're a sight for sore eyes, my dear. But is Jim here by any chance?" He was hoping for a negative reply. Maybe if Jim wasn't here, he could ask Mrs. Murphy for a few dollars.

"Jim? Yes, of course. He's upstairs in his room." She looked disappointed. "Come in dear."

She ushered him into the hallway and slowly climbed the stairs to lead the way. He tried not to watch her swaying figure in front of him. He'd need a few more drinks to blind the reality of that large bottom she had.

She knocked at the door, "Jim, your father is here."

"Who?"

"Your father."

They heard a few mumbled phrases trickle out and then, "Yeah, I'll be right there," Jim replied in a hoarse and raspy voice. They could hear him getting dressed.

Mrs. Murphy whispered to Red so that his son couldn't hear, "You could visit with me after if you like. I still have a little Sherry left. We could toast to the New Year. Don't be a stranger." With that invitation she kissed him on the cheek and went downstairs, blowing him another kiss.

He took another quick drink from his flask. Jim finally opened the door. He was dressed in an old black T-shirt and jeans. He looked terrible. He was unshaven and appeared to be recovering from a hangover. He hadn't had time to compose himself, Red observed.

"So how's my son?"

"Come on in and have a seat," Jim muttered.

The room was clean and well-organized unlike the last time Red was here. The television was on as usual to a baseball game, but the

The Visit

place looked dark and unlit. The window facing the street was open but there wasn't any breeze coming through. The carpet was a dark blue and worn in spots. The wall paper was faded. It was all a little depressing for Red, as he moved to the couch to sit down. He noticed the picture of Jim's mother, Nora, on the mantle piece under a painting. Nora was Red's first wife who died twenty five years ago on September 30. Red had married again, but Jim never seemed to accept his father's new wife, Mary.

Jim said, "So Dad, what's up?"

"To tell you the truth, I've had a drop or two. Excuse me son, but on my way here I passed Donovan's and because of the heat I had to have a couple of cool beers. It's hot out there in the sun, my boy."

Jim Kelly looked at his father mop the sweat from his forehead with a handkerchief. He noticed the corners of his father's mouth tasting the first touches of age. His eyes were puffy from drink.

"I've only come for a few minutes, Jim," he continued, looking at his son's brooding eyes that rested heavily upon him, "but on a highly important matter." He began fidgeting. "You see, son. Excuse me if I'm disturbing you but. . ."

Not for a moment did Jim try to erase the embarrassment and anxiety of his father. Jim sat down next to his father, his eyes dark and melancholy.

"Do you have twenty dollars you could lend me, son? Just a loan till Tuesday you understand. You see, it's your mother's birthday today and I don't have any money. Maybe I can get her some perfume or something. You know. . . She always likes those kinds of things."

Jim took out his wallet and handed his father the money without a word. With obvious relief in his voice his father relaxed, stuffing the money into his pocket.

"You're a good son, Jim, but it's been a long time since we've seen each other. How are you? You're looking all right. Are you getting along okay? You don't seem to be saying much. Are you listening? Sometimes, I think I am talking to myself. Aren't you glad to see your old man? I wanted to come see you sooner but I never could find the time. Oh it's no use. You know I'm lying, Jim. I've been out of work now for quite a while — just hanging around Donovan's Bar talking to the guys. Just killing time, I guess. There's not much work on the docks now."

"Dad, as I remember there was never much work on the docks."

"Well, you know, son, I was a very good worker. And the other guys were jealous of all the work I got done. It's all political. So when there was a big job opening up, I never got it."

"That's the way with everything, right, Dad?"

There was a moment of silence. Then Red, with a pained expression, sighed deeply.

"Is that a bottle I see over there?"

"Yeah, but it's empty."

"Aren't you going to offer me a beer or something, son?"

Jim went to the small refrigerator and took out two cans of beer. He opened them and gave one to his father. At the sight of the beer, Jim's father became animated.

"Yesterday they had the races on TV at Donovan's. Bill and Stingo were there. Ed came in for the bets and I couldn't resist it. Black Dancer had to win, so I put five dollars on the nose. Bill and Stingo started ribbin' the hell out of me. Damn it, that race was exciting. Black Dancer made his move at the stretch. What a drive! Fifth... fourth... third... second... then nose to nose with Sea Gull — the favorite. They crossed the wire. If he had only begun his drive just a few seconds sooner. Twelve to one odds — nothing to be sneezed at. Why, I could have been a millionaire. I've been watching that horse for months now. I tell you, he was due. Ah, if I had to give up the ponies, Jim, I'd go nuts. I couldn't survive. Do you understand me? Did you ever have anything like that happen to you, son?"

"I don't like the horses, remember?"

"Oh, yeah now that I think about it. I remember asking you once if you wanted to go to the track and you politely declined. Well, I guess you don't take after your old man that way."

The Visit

Again silence fell in the room. Red didn't like silence, "This foreign beer tastes kind of funny," he said. "What's the matter, don't you like American beer? This stuff is too bitter for me."

"After a while everything tastes bitter to you, Dad."

"You're the one who is bitter. I know how to enjoy life."

"You're hiding from life. You're always lying and cheating about everything."

"That's not true. Maybe I exaggerate a little, but that's my personality."

"Did you exaggerate a little when you told Mary you were going to quit drinking?"

"Listen I know how to take care of myself. Sometimes I need a drink just to get along with the likes of you. I want to have some fun in my life. I don't care what Mary and you think. The next thing you will be telling me is to go to A.A."

"Right, Dad, as if you'd go."

"I need to feel the joy of life."

"Didn't you tell Mary you would stop drinking, Dad?

"I don't want to talk about this no more."

"Okay, it's your life. Do what you want. You'll do what you want anyway."

"You're right. It's my life and I'll do what I want."

It was a drowsy Sunday afternoon and the light from outside made the room look lonely. Red looked restless and he walked to the mantlepiece. He took a long drink from his beer and twisted his mouth in distaste. Here he was in Jim's room and in the space of less than fifteen minutes they were at each other. He took another swig of beer and noticed Jim watching him.

"Don't look at me like that, Jim. By the way, are you still going out with that girl from another country?"

"Her name is Pearl and she's from Brazil."

"She's not for you, son. You should be going out with a beautiful Irish girl."

"She's the nicest thing that's happened to me in a long time and she's beautiful."

"It's good to stick to your own. Your mother Nora would have said the same thing."

Red spotted a book on the table, "That's a book on Yeats that I gave you. Did you finish it yet?"

"That's a book from Pearl. She gave it to me for my birthday. It's called, *How to Survive a Dysfunctional Family*."

"What is that a joke?"

Jim didn't reply.

Red looked at Nora's picture on the mantlepiece. He picked up the silver frame and kissed it. "A lovely lady she was. But Nora's gone now. Mary is your mother. Hey, where is a picture of Mary? I know what you're thinking. You're thinking that she's not really your mother, only a step-mother. But she's been taking care of you since you were eight years old. Surely, Mary has some claim as a mother. Some people blame me for Nora's death, but I know you don't. It's not your fault your mother died when you were being born, but that's the way life is."

Suddenly, a car's horn became stuck and the noise grated both men's nerves. Finally, it stopped.

"What's this I hear about your high and mighty ways?" Red almost yelled. "Stingo says that you feel that you're too good to live with your own family now just because you have a good paying job. I just don't understand you. Other children live at home with their family, but you, you're different. You think you're too good. You're too good to live with your brothers and sisters. We're your own flesh and blood. Are you ashamed of us? But don't worry, I wasn't born yesterday. Although Mrs. Murphy said that she doesn't allow any girls in your room, I know what goes on up here. You think that you can fool your father. Ha. . . that's a laugh. You have to get up pretty early to do that. I've seen you talking to these young girls in the street. You can't fool me."

"Damn it. . . you're my son, aren't you, Jim? Then for heaven's sake act like a son, and come on over to the house tonight. Eat some dinner with the family. Everyone will be happy to see you, Mary will be happy to see you."

"Listen, why don't you come home and live with us, with your mother, your brother and sisters? Now that you have a good paying job, you can help us out a little. Help us pay for the rent and the food unless you've gotten too high and mighty for us." Jim's father finished off the rest of his beer. He banged the empty can on the table.

Jim's face darkened for a moment.

"Come on, let's go to Donovan's first. The boys will be glad to see you and then we can go to the house. You aren't ashamed to be seen with your father now, are you? Let's go."

"You go. I'll meet you there."

They had been about an hour at the bar. Jim's father had bought the house a couple of rounds and was playing the part of the prodigal son's father. How many times did the phrase, "This is my long lost son returning to the fold in whom I am well pleased" turn up? Jim couldn't count. Needless to say the money that Red borrowed from Jim soon disappeared. As soon as this happened, old friends vanished and Jim's father pressed his son to come home and join him for a fine home-cooked dinner.

Soon they were out on the street. They walked up the block a few houses and entered a red-brick apartment house. The smell of garlic and cabbage permeated the hallway. The hallway was dark and the wood and carpet were in an advanced state of decay. A door was open at the end of the hallway.

"Mary, look who I drug up!"

A woman in her late thirties entered the living room.

"Oh, him. What's he want, a free meal?"

Jim couldn't help laughing, "I guess I do."

"I met him at Donovan's and he said he wanted to see everyone again — his beloved family. Where are the kids?" Red slurred his words.

"They're out as usual when it's time to have dinner. I see you've been to Donovan's again."

"A man has to have some kind of pleasure in this mean world. Don't be so hard on us, Mary."

Mary left the living room. Jim heard her shouting out the window for Erin and Timmy to come up for dinner.

"And here is my pride and joy," Red said pointing to a baby in a high chair, "Young Kathleen. Only a year old but smart as the devil." He winked and whispered in his son's ear. "Your mother's still got what it takes."

"Kathleen sure is cute. She looks just like you, Dad," Jim laughed.

"She better not look like me. It's Mary she looks like."

Mary returned, "And what are the likes of you two fussin' about in here? I can see that both of you are up to your old tricks again, huh? Where did you get the money to go drinking, Red?"

"Is that the way to talk now, Mary? Here I met him in the bar now and he said simply that he missed home and the family."

"Well, who told him to come here anyway? It was bad enough when he was living here all the time — just hanging around doing nothing all day. Now that he's got a job, he's too good to live here and give some of his earnings for food and rent to help the family. No... Jim gives it to Mrs. Murphy. He's too good for us now."

"Listen, Mary, the poor boy is homesick. He wants a good meal, a good substantial home-cooked meal. Now, what's the sin in that? Come on, son. Let's have a drink before the meal."

Suddenly Jim said, "Let's not have a drink before the meal. Why don't you tell Mary the truth?"

Mary laughed. "That's a new one! Your father telling the truth? Next you'll want him to go to church. What's this about the truth?"

"Oh Jim is just having some fun. There's nothing to tell. Unless it's to say that I love you."

"Listen, your malarkey won't work in this house any more, Red. We're on to you here. You drink too much. That's the truth. And Jim knows it."

Jim agreed. "She's got your number Dad."

Noises and shouts entered the living room as Erin, a twelve-year-old blonde, and Timmy, a ten-year-old scrawny boy with straight brown hair, raced to the kitchen.

"I beat you," cried Erin to Timmy.

Seeing Jim, she ran up to him and flung her arms around him. "We haven't seen you for so long."

"Hey, kiddo, I've missed you, too."

Erin pouted, "When are you going to take us to Prospect Park again?"

"Yeah," Timmy added. "We have to play some baseball."

Erin kissed him on the cheek and at the same time gave Timmy a shove to push him away. She wanted Jim to pay attention to her.

"Hey Jim," Timmy yelled, "my birthday's coming soon."

Erin gave him another push, so Timmy shouted, "Erin has a boyfriend. Erin let Johnny kiss her on the stairs. She thought that I wasn't looking. But I saw."

Mary immediately went up to Erin and took her by the arm.

"Don't let me hear of anything like that again, young lady. Didn't I just give you a little talk last week, you know what can happen."

"Oh, leave the poor girl alone, Mary. You were young before we married."

"Keep out of this, Red." Mary walked out of the room with Erin. Timmy followed them hoping Erin would get punished.

"Come on, Jim, maybe you had better go. Forget about the dinner for now. Mary's a little upset. It's that time of the month you know."

They both walked to the hallway. Jim could hear Kathleen crying.

"Listen, Jim. It's your mother's birthday and I had to buy some booze with the money you gave me at Donovan's and remember I think you had a drink or two. We couldn't show them that we were paupers, could we?"

Jim reached into his pocket and gave his father his last two twenty dollar bills.

"Come over to Donovan's sometime, Jim. I'm over there all the time. One of these days my horse will come in and we'll celebrate, huh?" He pressed his son's hand warmly. "It was good to see you again."

Jim walked out into the darkening street alone.